"I told you about Wesley. He's no bluff. He wants those blacks and he will have them. And he won't let anyone stand in his way. Not you. Not your missus." Harrod waited for a reply, but Nate was silent.

Nate glanced at the empty knife sheath on his hip as he crouched in his hiding place.

"I know how a coon like him thinks. He'll keep your woman alive only so long as it suits his purpose. Then he'll hand her over to the others. You haven't met them yet. They're animals. They'll gladly slit her throat after they've had their way."

An image of Winona enduring the unspeakable set Nate's blood to boiling. He grew warm all over and touched his belt where his flintlocks should be.

"I thought you cared for her," Harrod persisted.

Nate bit off an oath.

"The way you went on about how nice she is, and all, I didn't think you'd want them to do the kinds of things they're going to do to her. What will it be? Don't you want to spare your woman a fate worse than death?"

WILDERNESS #59: ONLY THE STRONG

David Thompson

LEISURE BOOKS   NEW YORK CITY

Dedicated to Judy, Joshua, and Shane.

A LEISURE BOOK®

March 2009

Published by

Dorchester Publishing Co., Inc.
200 Madison Avenue
New York, NY 10016

ISBN 10: 0-8439-6095-7
ISBN 13: 978-0-8439-6095-2
E-ISBN: 1-4285-0646-2

The name "Leisure Books" and the stylized "L" with design are trademarks of Dorchester Publishing Co., Inc.

Printed in the United States of America.

10 9 8 7 6 5 4 3 2 1

Visit us on the web at www.dorchesterpub.com.

WILDERNESS #59:
ONLY THE STRONG

Chapter One

They were seven rattlers on horseback.

They came out of the east, and the dawn, wending along the belt of green that fringed the Platte River. In the lead rode a hawk-faced man in buckskins, a fine Kentucky rifle in the crook of his arm. His eyes were as hard as flint. He missed nothing, this man. Not the deer that bounded off at their approach, not the buzzard that circled high in the sky, not the lowly sparrows that flitted and chirped in the undergrowth.

The man was a hunter by nature. As a boy he'd hunted everything that breathed. Rabbits, coons, squirrels, deer, boars, bear—all fell to his swift trigger finger. Now, as a man, he hunted a different kind of game. His quarry didn't have four legs; his quarry had two. He was a hunter of men. But only a certain type of men. Men—and women—with black skin.

He hunted runaway slaves.

Wesley was his name. That was all he went by. He always wore buckskins. He always had his rifle with him and a knife on his hip. Born and bred in the backwoods, he was a product of the forest.

Wesley was good at what he did. Never, in the

eight years he had been a slave hunter, had a slave escaped him. Until recently he worked for a man called Catfish. But now Catfish was dead and Wesley had struck off on his own, as much for the money the slaves would bring as for revenge; the slaves he was after were to blame for Catfish's death.

Behind Wesley came six others, the last leading packhorses. Some wore homespun and some wore store-bought clothes. They all bristled with weapons. Each was an armory and needed to be, given where they were and where they were headed.

It was the middle of the morning when Wesley came to a clearing and drew rein. In the center were the charred remains of a campfire. Dismounting, Wesley sank onto a knee and ran his fingers through the blackened bits of wood and ash. "We're a week behind, maybe less."

"Damn!" declared a man-mountain whose bushy tangle of a beard covered his entire chest. "I was hopin' we'd have gained by now."

"Patience, Trumbo," Wesley said to his friend and partner. "We must be patient."

A third man, the youngest, a bundle of nerves in a floppy black hat, gray shirt and brown pants, swore. "Patience, hell. I figured on catching them by now. At the rate we're going, we'll be lucky to do it before they reach the Rockies."

"Here or there, it's all the same," Wesley said. "You need to work on your patience, too, Cranston."

Cranston frowned. The day was hot and the heat did not help his temper. "The last thing I need is someone telling me what I need."

Wesley stood and turned, and when he stopped turning his Kentucky rifle was pointed at the younger man's head. "I'm tired of your carping."

"Now listen—"

"No. *You* listen. Learn to curb that tongue of yours, or you can head on back."

Cranston blinked and gestured. "By my lonesome? Are you addlepated? We're hundreds of miles from the Mississippi, in the middle of the prairie, for God's sake."

"Kit Carson could make it back. Daniel Boone could make it. *I* could make it."

"You were born in the woods. You're at home in these wilds." Cranston gazed with distaste about them. "Trees and grass, grass and trees, that's all we've seen for days. Give me a city or town."

The next rider, short of stature and broad with muscle, grunted in agreement. "You have your talents, Wesley, and we have ours. It's why you hired us."

"I hired you and your friends, Olan, because you kill for money. But don't make the mistake of thinking Trumbo or I won't do our own killing when there's some to be done."

"You hired us for our lack of scruples? I'm shocked." Olan grinned as he said it.

Wesley allowed himself a rare smile. "I asked around. They say you will kill anyone, anytime, with no qualms. Best of all, they say that when you take a job, you see it through."

"We've never disappointed anyone yet."

The last man, the one leading their packhorses, was at least twenty years older than the rest. He wore greasy buckskins. He had overheard, and he called out, "What about me, slave hunter? Trumbo, there, is your pard. Olan and Cranston and Bromley and Kleist blow out wicks. But why did you hire me?"

"You, Harrod?" Wesley stepped to his mount. "I hired you because you have something the rest don't."

"What would that be?"

"Experience. You know the prairie and the mountains."

"That I do," Harrod agreed with a bob of his salt-and-pepper chin. "I got the itch back when beaver plews fetched good money."

Wesley went to respond, but just then the brush rustled and out stepped several Indians. Instantly, he trained his Kentucky on them. Everyone else, with the exception of Harrod, jerked their rifles to their shoulders.

"Don't shoot!" the old frontiersman yelled. "They're harmless. They're only Otoes."

There were two men and a woman. The men wore leggings but no shirts. Their black hair was cropped short at the front and on the sides, but they had long braids at the back. All had high cheekbones and low foreheads. The men were armed with bows but had not notched arrows to the strings.

The woman stayed back, her face shyly averted. A doeskin dress fell to below her knees.

"They're friendly, you say?" Wesley asked.

"None friendlier, unless it's the Shoshones," Harrod answered. "They farm some, they hunt some, they leave whites be."

Olan was admiring the woman. "It's been weeks since I had me a female."

"They're friendly, I say," Harrod repeated.

"I can be right friendly, too."

One of the warriors went up to Wesley and smiled. His hands flowed in expressive movements.

"That there is sign language," Harrod said. "Nearly all the tribes use it to talk."

"What is he saying?"

"His name is High-backed Wolf. He greets his white brothers and asks if we have coffee to spare."

"White brother, am I?" Wesley said, and raising his Kentucky, he shot High-backed Wolf in the face.

For a few seconds the other two Otoes were frozen with shock. Then the other warrior snatched at his quiver, but he had just started to draw an arrow out when several rifles thundered at once and he was jolted backward by the impact of multiple slugs.

The woman put the back of her hand to her mouth, her eyes wide with terror, and wheeled to flee. She only managed a couple of steps before Olan brought his horse up next to her and brought the stock of his rifle crashing down.

"God in heaven!" Harrod exclaimed. "What the hell did you do that for? I told you they were friendly."

Wesley stared at the blood oozing from the hole below High-backed Wolf's right eye. "Get this straight, old man. I'm not anyone's brother unless they're white." Leaning his Kentucky against his leg, Wesley uncapped his powder horn. "I can't abide the lower races."

"Lower?"

"The red race. The black race. The yellow race. You name it." Wesley poured powder into his palm. "Why do you think I do what I do?"

"I figured it was for the money. Or maybe you were one of those who likes the thrill of the hunt."

"There's that. But the main reason I became a slave hunter is because I can't stand blacks. I can't stand how they look. I can't stand how they talk. I can't stand their stink. If it were up to me, I'd wipe out every damn darkie."

Olan chuckled. "A man after my own heart."

"I didn't know," Harrod said.

"Now you do. From here on out, every redskin we come across I'll kill, unless there are too many of them."

"I see. And these slaves we're after? The Worth family? Do you plan to kill them, too?"

"Be sensible. The bounty is for dead or alive, but it's a lot more for alive. That's how I'll take them back so long as they don't give me cause to curl up their toes."

"I see," Harrod said again. He nodded at the woman, who had groaned and was stirring. "What about her?"

"She's Olan's to do with as he pleases."

Olan licked his thin lips. "Now this is the kind of job I like. Kleist, fetch some water from the river so we can bring her around. Cranston, Bromley, climb down and hold her arms and legs. She's apt to claw and kick."

Harrod gigged his horse toward the other side of the clearing.

"Where do you think you're going?" Wesley wanted to know.

"I'd rather not watch."

Olan scowled. "What is this, old man? Don't tell me you're some kind of Injun lover?"

"I don't give any more of a hoot about red skin than I do about white," Harrod said. "But I do give a hoot about females. I can't stand to see them abused. It's the one thing I'll not abide."

"Well, I'll be," Olan said.

Cranston laughed and shook his head. "It takes all kinds, doesn't it?" He trained his rifle on the frontiersman's back. "I ought to blow you to hell, you old goat."

"We need him," Wesley said.

"But you heard," Cranston objected. "He's got a soft spot. Me, I lost my grandpa and an uncle to red vermin, and I'd as soon shoot anyone who sides with them."

Wesley raised his Kentucky. "I don't make a habit of repeating myself, boy. Harrod is not to be touched. I have a special use for him."

Cranston hesitated, and then saw that Trumbo had pointed his rifle at him, too. Shrugging, he said, "Whatever you say, Mister. You're paying us. But I should think you'd agree with me, hating Injuns and blacks like you do."

"There's a time and a place, boy. We have to know when to keep our hate in and when to let it out." Wesley nodded at Harrod. "You can go on ahead if you want but don't go far."

The frontiersman jabbed his heels into his horse. He rode several hundred yards and drew rein on a grassy bank overlooking a pool. Climbing down, he sat with his legs dangling over the side and stared at the water.

After a few moments hooves thudded, and Harrod pushed to his feet. He didn't hide his surprise. "I reckoned you would stay and take part."

"Not me," Wesley said, alighting with agile grace. "Her kind don't appeal to me."

"Your partner, Trumbo?"

"He's not as particular."

Harrod gnawed his lower lip until he couldn't hold in what he wanted to say. "Mind if I ask you a question?"

"Only if you don't mind if I don't answer."

"Fair enough." Harrod sat back down. "These blacks we're after, the Worth family."

"What about them."

"You told me they're runaway slaves, but you never told me *why* they ran away. Is it that they want to be free? I've heard that a good many Negroes try to reach Northern states like Pennsylvania and New York."

"You heard true," Wesley confirmed.

"Then why are these Worths heading west? Why try and reach the Rockies when it makes more sense for them to do the same as other runaway slaves?"

Wesley puffed a speck of dust from his rifle. "They're not running for their freedom. They're running for their lives."

"Care to explain?"

Squatting, Wesley balanced his rifle across his knees and regarded the flowing water. "These Worths did the worst thing slaves can do: They killed their master."

"Does that happen often?"

"Hardly ever. They worked on a plantation run by Frederick Sullivan and his two sons, Brent and Justin. Brent took a shine to Randa Worth and her pa went and murdered him."

"I see."

"You say that a lot," Wesley said.

Harrod gnawed on his lower lip some more. "Mind if I ask you another question?"

"Damned if you ain't the most curious son of a bitch I ever ran across. What now?"

"You made mention of some people who are helping the Worths. Who are they? And what do we do when we catch them?"

"The Worths are being helped by a mountain man and his squaw. It was them who killed the man I worked for, a gent known as Catfish, the best slave hunter there ever was. They'll pay for that. They'll pay in blood. But first I intend for them to suffer. I want to hear them beg for their lives before I snuff out their wicks."

"I see."

"You only think you do."

"This mountain man and his wife—do you happen to know their names?"

"Nate and Winona King."

Chapter Two

The girl was young and black and full of life. She had on a store-bought dress, the first store-bought dress she ever owned. If it were up to her she would keep it locked in a trunk and put it on only for special occasions. But her mother insisted she wear it to show the man and woman who bought it for her that she truly liked it, and the girl always did as her mother wanted her to do.

Randa Worth would wear it, but she refused to let it get dirty. Every smudge, every smear, every particle of dirt, she washed off. At night she shook the dress out, neatly folded it, and slept with it under her blanket, where it would be safe.

On this particular evening, Randa had been sipping tea when she spilled some on the dress. She promptly put the tin cup down and hurried to the river. The Platte River, they told her it was called.

Sinking to her knees, Randa dipped her hands in the water and splashed some on the spots the tea had made. Not that she thought the tea would leave stains; she wasn't taking any chances with the prettiest dress she'd ever owned, though.

Randa's reflection stared back at her from the surface of the Platte. She hadn't changed much in the weeks they had been on the trail. To look at her, a person would never suspect the changes she was going through.

Her mother said every girl her age went through them, but Randa wasn't sure she liked them. She certainly didn't want her bosom to become as big as her mother's, yet there was no denying that where she had once had walnuts, she now had apples.

"Why couldn't I stay as I was?" Randa asked her reflection, and bent to dip her hand in again.

Suddenly the brush rustled and crackled, and the next instant a monster lumbered into sight. Or so it seemed to Randa. She had never seen a buffalo this close before. A bull buffalo, over five feet tall at the shoulder, with curved horns that made Randa think of twin sickles. She shuddered at the thought of them ripping into her body, and she cupped her wet hand to her mouth to holler to the others for help.

But Randa didn't yell. She had changed her mind. So far the buffalo was ignoring her. Maybe it didn't realize she was there. A yell might provoke it to charge.

Randa couldn't get over how big it was. She had seen cows and oxen and hogs back on the plantation, but they were puny compared to this beast. Or maybe it was her imagination. Maybe it only looked so enormous because it was so close. Maybe it really wasn't as scary as she thought it was.

Then the great behemoth of the plains swiveled its giant head and stared at her, and Randa felt goose bumps ripple down her spine. It really *was* scary, and when its nostrils flared and it snorted, Randa did what her instincts compelled her to do: She rose, whirled, and ran.

And Randa could run. Ever since she was knee

high to her mother, she'd been extremely swift of foot. She proved it by winning many of the races the slaves held. She'd always wanted to enter the races the whites put on, but it wasn't allowed. Slaves were not allowed to mix socially with their masters.

Randa flew, her bare feet smacking the earth so lightly and rapidly that she barely touched the ground.

But as fast as she was, the buffalo was faster.

She heard it crashing through the vegetation after her, and she glanced back to discover, to her horror, that its size did not mean it was slow. To the contrary, its massive muscles propelled it after her as if it were a hairy cannonball shot from a cannon.

"Oh God!" Randa blurted, and applied all the speed her sinews could muster. The cottonwoods and other trees were a blur. She was running blindly, desperately, and it occurred to her that wasn't the thing to do. She should run for help. She should make for the clearing where she had left her ma and pa and brother, and the Kings. Nate King, in particular, would know what to do. The mountain man knew everything there was to know about the prairie and the animals that called the prairie their home.

The buffalo narrowed the space between them. Every breath was a wheeze as loud as a blacksmith's bellows. The thud of its heavy hooves was like the beat of drums.

Randa glanced back again and gasped. It was so close! Its black horns bobbed with every bound, and she imagined them hooking her and rending her poor body limb from limb. "Please, no," she said.

Randa faced front. Too late, she saw the bush. She didn't know what kind it was, only that it was a tangle of small vinelike limbs, and when she slammed into them, they wrapped around her legs. Before she could stop or veer to the side, her feet were swept out from under her and she crashed down on her shoulder. Instantly, Randa went to push up and keep running, but a gigantic silhouette loomed above her, and she turned to stone.

The bull straddled her. Out of the corner of her eye, Randa saw its gaze fixed intently on her. It sniffed her and pawed the ground. Its warm breath fanned her arm, her cheek. She was nose to nostrils with one of the most fearsome creatures on the continent, and she bit her lip to keep from screaming.

"Don't move!"

Randa's gaze darted to the man who had rushed up. She almost cried out his name in heartfelt relief.

Nate King was big in his own right. Big and broad of shoulder, his muscular frame clothed in buckskins and moccasins. A powder horn and ammo pouch crisscrossed his chest. A possibles bag hung at his side. Twin flintlock pistols were wedged under his wide brown leather belt, and a bowie knife in a beaded sheath hung on his left hip. On his right hip was a tomahawk. In his hands, trained on the bull buffalo, was a Hawken rifle custom made for him by the famed brothers of that name in St. Louis. A beaver hat contained his black mane of hair, and a single white eagle feather hung from the back of his head.

"Don't move," Nate cautioned a second time. "It's only curious. If it were mad, you'd be dead by now."

The buffalo raised its shaggy head and stared at him. Nate fingered his Hawken but didn't shoot. His wife came running to his side and wedged her rifle to her shoulder.

"Don't fire unless it charges, Winona."

Winona was a Shoshone. A fine doeskin dress, decorated with scores of blue beads, hung to below her knees. Like Nate, she had a powder horn, ammo pouch and hunting knife. Like Nate, she was armed with a brace of pistols and held a Hawken. And like her man, she showed no fear as she took deliberate aim.

"If it charges, go for the lungs."

"I have killed buffalo before, Husband. You might recall—you were there when I shot some of them."

Nate had specified the lungs for a reason. Buffalo skulls were so thick that penetrating them to the brain was next to impossible. A heart or lung shot was best, and even then the lead ball must shear through thick layers of fat and muscle to reach the vitals. Next to grizzlies and gluttons, buffalo were about the hardest creatures to kill of any alive.

Other figures came running: a black man almost as big as Nate, a woman as wide as she was tall, and a boy of fourteen. Samuel Worth; his wife, Emala; and their son, Chickory. All three stopped when Nate motioned.

"Randa!" Emala cried.

"Hush, woman!" Samuel Worth snapped. "Do you want to get our girl killed?"

Chickory grabbed his father's arm. "What do we do, Pa? What do we do?"

"You do nothing," Nate King said. "Stand still and keep quiet and maybe it will leave her be."

"Maybe?"

The bull sniffed loudly at Randa's face and neck. A drop of saliva fell on her cheek, and she quivered.

"Stay still!" Nate stressed.

Randa was trying, but her body wouldn't stop trembling.

Nate edged forward. The girl was doing her best but might give in to fear at any moment. He'd encountered buffs before, and nine times out of ten, when confronted by a human, they ran. It was the tenth time he had to worry about.

The bull snorted. It stamped. Just when it seemed it would charge, it wheeled and crashed off through the undergrowth.

"Praise the Lord!" Emala exclaimed.

Nate was the first to reach Randa, and he helped her up. "Are you all right? Did it hurt you any?"

Randa, trembling, sagged against him, her cheek on his broad chest. "Thank you, thank you, thank you."

Nate patted her shoulder. "There, there. You did fine. Exactly as you should have."

"I did?"

Winona joined them. Only a few steps behind were Chickory, Samuel and Emala.

Emala pried Randa from Nate and practically enfolded her daughter in her motherly bosom. "Lordy! Don't scare us like that, child. I was prayin' like I've never prayed. That awful creature, with all that hair and those horns! Why the Good Lord made such a thing, only the Good Lord knows."

Samuel offered his calloused hand to Nate. "I'm sorry you have to keep savin' us, Mr. King. I thank you again."

Nate shook Samuel's hand heartily. He liked the Worths, liked them a lot. It was partly why he agreed to guide them to the Rockies. The other part had to do with the slaver hunters who had been after them.

Two-legged coyotes who hurt Winona when she tried to help the Worths. No one hurt Nate's wife and got away with it. *Ever*.

Chickory was staring after the buffalo. "Did you see how big that thing was? And you say there's millions of them? How can that be? Are they like rabbits, always havin' young?"

Nate explained, "The cows usually only have one calf at a time. I reckon there are so many because they can live twenty-five years or better, and there's not much that can kill them except man." Wolves weeded out the old and the sick, but they were relatively few.

"It's the Almighty's doin'," Emala declared. "His hand is over this land. It's the Garden of Eden all over again."

Nate read the Bible often. He loved to read. In their cabin was an entire shelf lined with books, his most prized possessions. "The Garden of Eden had the Tree of Life and every animal under the sun."

Emala brightened. "You know your Scripture."

"When my children were little, I read passages to them every night."

"So did I. I admire that in a man," Emala said with a pointed look at her husband. "Ask my family and they'll tell you that I'm the God-fearin'est female who ever lived."

"Ain't that the truth," Chickory said.

"Amen, Son," Samuel threw in.

Emala frowned. "You and me are havin' words tonight when we're alone."

"What are you mad about now?"

"Nothin'."

"Then why do you look fit to kick me?"

Nate couldn't get over how much they squabbled.

Emala was particular about things, and when they weren't done to suit her, she let whomever displeased her know it. It made him appreciate Winona all the more. Oh, she lit into him now and again and nagged him on occasion, but mostly she let him do as he felt best without constantly criticizing him.

Randa clasped Nate's hand. "You sure were wonderful, Mr. King."

"I hardly did anything," Nate assured her, and was puzzled when his wife grinned.

"You stood up to that buffalo as bold as could be." Randa heaped on the praise. "The same as when you helped us against those slave hunters."

"A man does what he has to." Nate didn't know what else to say. He tried to pull his hand back but she held on.

"You killed three of them to save us," Randa gushed. "You were"—she stopped, searching for the right word—"magnificent."

Emala snatched her daughter's wrist. "Come on, girl." She nearly yanked Randa off her feet. "Let's get you back to the fire, where it's safe."

Nate watched them walk off and became aware that his wife was staring at him and still grinning. "What?"

"My, you are a handsome devil," Winona said in her flawless English. She had a talent for learning languages that far surpassed his own.

"What are you talking about?"

"You do not see it, and it is right in front of your face."

"What?"

"Is that the only word you know today?" Winona made a show of trying to remember something. "Now, let me see. What is it our daughter-in-law likes to say about men? Oh, yes." She paused. "As blind as bats and as dumb as tree stumps." She laughed gaily.

"Why is it," Nate asked, "that women feel the need to talk rings around a man before they get to the point?"

"My point, dear husband, is that sweet Randa is smitten. Ever since you saved them from those slave hunters, her eyes follow you everywhere. Surely you've noticed?"

No, Nate hadn't, and he decided to change the subject. "It's too bad I didn't kill all of them."

"Why? Do you think the two who got away will make more trouble for the Worths?"

"I hope not. I hope they have the brains to leave well enough be. But Samuel told me there's a bounty on their heads. Thousands of dollars. That pair might not give up."

"What will you do if they come after us?"

"Need you ask?" Nate King said.

Chapter Three

Emala Worth would tell you she wasn't the bravest of souls. Truth was, Emala was timid. She was scared of so many things, she had lost count. Spiders, snakes, mice, rats, mosquitoes, bees, wasps, lightning, big dogs, bulls and even cows. She was afraid of horses, too, although she was gradually getting over her fear of them after weeks of riding across the prairie.

But one thing Emala couldn't get over, one fear she couldn't escape, was her dread of the wilderness. There was so much to be afraid of, it was as if the Good Lord deliberately put the wilderness there just to scare people to death. Bears, wolves, cougars, hostiles, you name it, the wild haunts crawled with them. And from what the Kings told her, the mountains weren't any better.

Buffalo were at the top of Emala's to-be-afraid-of list. They were so *big* and so hairy, and those horns were like swords. It didn't help that they had bad tempers. She couldn't help comparing them to her husband, who was prone to lose his temper now and again.

Emala's heart had leaped into her throat at the sight of her precious daughter being menaced by that mean bull. Of all her many fears, her greatest was that she would lose one of her children. They were everything to her. It was partly out of love for Randa that Emala agreed to flee the plantation even though her heart wasn't in it.

Some folks would say she was crazy. They would say that being a slave was the worst thing you could be. But being a slave was all Emala ever knew. She was born into slavery, just as her mother before her. To her, their small shack and pitifully few possessions were as good as life got, and she never hankered after more.

It helped that Emala had refuge in her faith. She believed in the Lord God Almighty. She'd read the Bible completely through and was proud of the feat. When her children were little, in the evenings she would read to them to instill her love of Scripture in them.

Leaving her Bible behind when they fled had been the hardest thing Emala ever did. She missed it. She missed it terribly. And now, winding along the Platte River, she grew sad with regret. So sad, she didn't notice when her horse acquired a shadow.

"Is something the matter?"

Emala gave a start. "Mr. King! You about scared me out of a year's growth."

Nate was astride his big bay, his Hawken in the crook of his elbow. "You looked fit to cry."

"I am," Emala confessed. She explained, ending with, "I can do without a lot of things, but I can't do without my Scripture."

"Maybe I can help," Nate offered. "Remember my little library I mentioned?"

"I surely do." Emala had always wanted to own more books but what little money she earned back on the plantation went for more important things.

"I have a Bible. In fact, I have two. One was my mother's. I brought it back with me from my last trip to New York City. The other one I bought in St. Louis. I had a third, a Bible that belonged to my Uncle Zeke, but I lost it when some men broke into our cabin."

"They destroyed your Bible?"

"And all my other books. It took me a long time to replace them."

"Any man who would do that to the Word of the Lord should be burned at the stake." Emala paused. "Your Uncle Zeke, you say? Isn't he the one who brought you out here? He was goin' to teach you all there was to know about livin' in the mountains, but then he went and died on you, right?"

"Uncle Zeke was killed by the Kiowas, yes. Fortunately, a friend of his came along and became my mentor, you might say. Shakespeare McNair." Nate gazed up the trail. "The point of all this is that I have a Bible to spare. When we reach King Valley, I'll give it to you."

"Oh, I couldn't take your Bible." Emala was genuinely shocked. She was used to whites treating her pretty much as they treated their cattle. But Nate and Winona had been kind to them from the start. The Kings bought them clothes and weapons, and, wonder of wonders, not only offered to guide them to the Rocky Mountains, but invited them to come live in the same valley.

Emala never imagined white folks could be so nice. She'd noticed that Nate never cussed, which was a miracle in itself. It was her experience that cussing came as natural to men as breathing. Even her Samuel, no matter how much she nagged him, couldn't control his tongue.

Then there was Winona. Emala had never met an honest-to-goodness Indian woman before. Somehow, Emala got it into her head that all Indians lived for, male and female, was to lift the hair of every white—and black—they came across. But Winona was about the sweetest lady Emala ever met, and about the strongest. No so much physically strong as strong inside. Emala envied her. She would have liked to be as strong, but it just wasn't in her.

Suddenly Emala became aware Nate was still talking.

". . . sitting on the shelf gathering dust. I'd be obliged if you would reconsider."

"It might take us forever to repay you."

"Who asked you to? It's enough that the book will be in the hands of someone who appreciates it." Nate smiled and reached out and touched her arm, then jabbed his heels and trotted on ahead.

"What a fine man," Emala murmured.

Not ten seconds later Samuel took his place. "What were you two talkin' about just now?"

"Why, Husband, you almost sound jealous," Emala teased.

"Be serious, woman. What is there to be jealous about? Nate's wife is the prettiest female I ever set eyes on. He's not about to throw her over for the likes of you."

Emala's blood began to boil. "Please, no more compliments. I don't think I can stand the praise."

Samuel cocked his head. "Listen to yourself. You're being silly. All I'm sayin' is that Nate King is happy with the woman he's got."

"How about you?"

"Me? How did I get into this?"

"Are you happy with the woman you've got? Sometimes you don't act like you are."

Wagging a finger at her, Samuel said, "No, you don't. You're not turnin' this around and blamin' me for God knows what."

"I wish you wouldn't take the Lord's name in vain. When we get to the pearly gates, He's liable to turn you away."

"Don't start on me with your religion."

"It's your religion too. Or have you gone and given up on God just as you gave up on our life on the plantation?"

Samuel squirmed as if fit to burst. "If you call wantin' a new and better life for my family giving up, then yes, I guess I gave up. Maybe you didn't mind havin' a yoke around your neck every minute of every day, but I did."

"You always make it out to be worse than it was."

"And you always make it out to be better. It's just plain silly."

"Well," Emala said.

They were silent for a space, and then Emala said, "What's happenin' to us? We never argued this much before we became runaways."

"I don't rightly know," Samuel admitted. "But it seems as if we can't hardly talk anymore without fightin'."

Emala was about to say that despite all their spatting, she still cared for him as deeply as ever, when she became aware that Nate King had stopped and raised an arm to signal them to do the same. "What is it, do you suppose?"

Nate said something to Chickory, who turned and whispered to Randa, who turned and whispered to Emala.

"Mr. King says there are a bunch of Indians yonder, and they might be hostiles."

"Lordy!" Emala exclaimed in horror. She could practically feel the sharp sting of a knife slitting her throat from ear to ear. "Is there no end?"

Nate King heard her and almost turned to tell her to hush, but she fell quiet. He concentrated on the figures moving about in a clearing ahead. By their features and their scalp locks and how they had fashioned their buckskins, he determined they were Pawnees.

Considered a friendly tribe, the Pawnees were some of the first to venture east of the Mississippi River to visit the land of the white men. They were quick to see that trade with the whites was to their advantage. Years ago, Pawnee chiefs met with President Jefferson. Later on, about twenty of them paid President Monroe a visit and put on a war dance at the White House.

But for all their friendliness, the Pawnees had a dark side. They were known to practice human sacrifice. Young female captives were offered up to the morning star in the belief it brought good fortune.

Other tribes distrusted them, which was not unusual since many tribes were suspicious of one another. But distrust of the Pawnees ran particularly deep. They had a reputation for being bloodthirsty. There was even a Shoshone saying to the effect that a Pawnee would smile as he greeted you while stabbing you in the back.

"Do we go around?" Winona asked. She held her Hawken across her saddle with her thumb on the hammer and her finger on the trigger.

Nate counted nine Pawnees altogether. Since two

were warriors and two were women and five were young ones ranging in age from ten about to about twenty, he reckoned it to be two families. They'd erected temporary shelters and were drying buffalo meat and curing hides.

Winona was looking about. "I only see these, but there could be others."

Nate scanned both sides of the Platte. "I think it's just them."

Unlike other plains tribes, the Pawnees did not rely on the buffalo for their existence. They hunted the beasts now and then, but mostly they farmed. They raised squash and maize and beans and other crops.

"Do we go around?" Winona asked again.

Nate shook his head. He doubted the two warriors would do anything with their families there.

"I hope you know what you are doing."

Nate hoped so, too. The last time he had dealings with the Pawnees, they tried to kill him. He gigged his bay, his Hawken at his side.

A young boy playing with a hoop made of sticks was the first to spot him, and shouted in alarm. Instantly, the two warriors grabbed rifles and moved in front of their wives and children to protect them.

Nate smiled to show he was friendly and called out in English, "We come in peace." In Shoshone, on the off chance they understood it, he said, "We want to be friends."

One of the warriors had streaks of gray in his hair and a seamed face that showed as clearly as words that he was a man who had seen and done much in his lifetime. His eyes glinted with intelligence. "We like peace, white man."

Nate drew rein. Winona did likewise. Then the

Worths emerged, and it was all Nate could do not to laugh.

The Pawnees were astounded. Their mouths fell, and the eyes of the young ones nearly bugged out of their heads. One of the women exclaimed something in the Pawnee tongue.

Nate reckoned they had never seen blacks before. He remembered when the Shoshones first set eyes on a black man, and how they touched his skin and his hair, marveling in childlike wonder at the difference between his and their own.

The warrior with the gray streaks bobbed his chin at the Worths. "These are the black white men I have heard of?"

Nate wasn't sure how to answer that. "They are black, yes. They are not black whites. They are black blacks."

"Petalesharo saw blacks many winters ago. He said they have hair like buffalo and their skin is like the night. Some of our people did not believe him, but now I see with my own eyes that he spoke true."

Nate vaguely recalled hearing of a Pawnee warrior by that name who went east of the Mississippi to see "the great white Father." "You speak the white tongue well."

"I speak three. The tongue of my people, your tongue, and the French tongue."

Nate realized that here was another linguist, like his wife. He had been shocked when he first discovered how much better she was at learning new languages. It was his fist true inkling of her keen intelligence. She was much more intelligent than he was. Yet she still loved him. Now, there was a miracle if ever there was one.

The Pawnee had gone on. "I have done much

trading with whites. And a white man lived with my people two winters. He taught me much of your tongue." The warrior drew himself up to his full height. "I am Pahaatkiwako. In your tongue I would be called Red Fox."

"I'm called Grizzly Killer."

Red Fox did not hide his sudden interest. "You are the white Shoshone? Your name is known among my people. You have killed many of the silver bears." He paused. "You have killed Chaticks-si-Chaticks."

Nate tensed. That was what the Pawnee called themselves. It meant "men of men," or something like that. "I kill only those who try to kill me. The Pawnees I killed were trying to spill my blood. I hope you won't hold it against me."

For all of a half minute the issue hung in the balance. The warrior's inscrutable face gave no clue to what he was thinking. Then he smiled and opened his arms wide, saying, "I am Pahaatkiwako of the Chaui, a Hunter, and I welcome you."

Nate was relieved. If he recollected rightly, the Pawnees were divided into four clans, of which the Chaui were one, although he couldn't remember what the word meant. He did know that the men further divided themselves into Hunters or Warriors. The former spent much of their time killing game to feed the mouths of their people, while the latter saw to village defense and went on frequent raids. "I am honored to meet you, Red Fox." He introduced Winona and the Worths.

"My heart will be warm, Grizzly Killer, if you will share our fire this night. We have much meat and maize. You will not go hungry."

Nate was tempted. They were making good time in their passage across the prairie. It wouldn't hurt to stop early for once and spend an evening in pleasant company. He didn't think for a moment that Red Fox was up to no good. And besides, he would take turns with Winona sitting up, just in case. "Let me put it to a vote." Wheeling his bay, he asked, "What will it be?" His question was directed at the Worths.

Samuel answered first. "If you think it's safe, Mr. King, we'll do whatever you say is best."

"It will be nice to meet other people," Randa said.

Chickory was staring at a Pawnee girl about his age. She, in turn, was fascinated by his hair. "I don't mind."

Emala bit her lower lip. "I don't know about this. Are you sure they're friendly? They won't scalp us in our sleep?"

Red Fox overheard, and chuckled. "We do not lift the hair of women. You need not fear."

"In that case, if everyone else is for it, I'm for it, too." Emala gave a nervous titter. "What harm can it do?"

Chapter Four

Wesley was on one knee, intent on tracks he was studying. "We're barely a day behind. If we push all night, by this time tomorrow we'll have them."

The six men on their horses behind him looked at one another. They were worn and weary and four of them were more than a little angry.

Olan was the angriest. Jabbing a finger at the backwoodsman, he said sourly, "You better be joshing. If you expect us to ride all night, you're addlepated."

Without taking his gaze from the tracks, Wesley said, "Is something the matter? I'm paying good money for your services."

"I won't argue that. But all the money in creation won't do us a lick of good if we ride ourselves and our animals into the ground. Hell, we haven't had more than two to three hours' sleep a night for the past ten days. We need to rest if we're to go up against that mountain man and his squaw. They're holy terrors. You said so yourself."

"I'm with Olan," Bromley said. Of middling height and build, he was distinguished by a bristly mustache and an English-made shotgun he hardly ever put down. "As hard as you're pushing us, we'd be easy pickings."

Trumbo kneed his mount up next to Wesley and reined around so he faced the others. "You'll do as Wes says, and like it," he rumbled, his rifle trained in the direction of the malcontents.

Olan bristled. "Don't threaten us. Not ever. You can pay us to take lead, but we'll be damned if we'll stand for any of that."

"He's right," young Cranston said.

Kleist, the quiet, grim German, gigged his horse up next to Olan's. Cranston and Bromley were quick to follow suit, so that the four of them formed a crescent around Wesley and Trumbo.

Trumbo hefted his rifle and glanced nervously at the backwoodsman, who had not gotten up off his knee.

Olan shifted in his saddle. "What about you, Harrod? Do you stand with them or do you stand with us?"

The grizzled, greasy frontiersman had stayed well back, with the packhorse. "Don't rope me into this. I don't like riding all day and most of every night, either. But when he hired me, Wesley told me we'd have to ride hard and fast. And since he's paying me more than I would get for most guide work, I reckon I'll do whatever he wants."

It was then that Wesley slowly rose and just as slowly turned. "Thank you for your confidence, Harrod. And Trumbo, for your loyalty. As for the rest of you—" They all heard the click of the Kentucky's hammer, "I'm beginning to regret hiring you. You came highly recommended as man killers but you fall short in a lot of other ways."

"Name one," Olan said indignantly.

"You can't track worth a lick. You can't live off the land unless a deer or a rabbit comes up and asks to be shot. You whine about the heat. You whine about the dust. You whine about going without sleep." Wesley pointed the Kentucky at him. "Is there anything I've missed?"

"Hold on, there," said Olan.

"There are four of us and only two of you," Cranston said.

Wesley sighed. "Boy, I have a rifle and two pistols and a knife besides. And if it comes to it, I'll rip out your throat with my teeth."

"I'd like to see you try."

"Shut up, damn you!" Olan snapped. He was staring at the Kentucky's muzzle. "Listen, woodsman. It could be I let my temper get the better of me."

"No 'could be' about it," Wesley said. "So I won't hold you to account *this* time. But if there's a next, I'll have to rethink whether you're worth the aggravation."

Cranston went to say something, but Olan suddenly leaned over and punched his arm.

"Not a word, you infant!"

Wesley lowered the Kentucky slightly. "I admit this has been rough on all of us. But it's either push hard now or chase the darkies all the way to the Rocky Mountains."

"That could take weeks," Olan said.

"We sure as hell don't want that," Bromley remarked.

"Then quit your bellyaching. The next time you—" Wesley stopped in midsentence.

The reason was Trumbo, who had raised a big arm and was pointing to the west. "Look yonder! Is that what I think it is?"

The sun was setting. Only the crown had yet to slip into the nether realm of impending night. And there, barely distinguishable against the backsplash of yellow and pink, was a tiny finger of orange.

"A campfire, you reckon?"

Wesley sniffed like a bloodhound trying to pick up a scent. "Wood smoke. They must have stopped for some reason."

"Everyone makes mistakes," Olan said.

"The mountain man hasn't yet. So let's not put the cart before the horse. Maybe it's someone else. A lot of folks cross the prairie this time of year. Or it could be redskins."

"We should wait until midnight, when all of them will most likely be asleep, and sneak up on them," Cranston suggested.

"All seven of us?" Wesley scoffed. "Sneak up on a mountain man without him hearing us?"

"You said it might not be him."

Bromley said, "We can be quiet as mice when we need to be."

"But can you be *quieter* than mice?" Wesley asked.

"That ain't possible."

"It is if you know how." Wesley regarded each of them in turn. "Do any of you have any notion what kind of man we're up against? I'm not talking about the slaves. They don't have the brains God gave a squirrel, and their senses are as dull as a turnip's. I'm talking about the mountain man."

"You said it might not be him," Cranston repeated.

"Why all this fuss over one man?" Olan threw in. "He puts his britches on one leg at a time just like the rest of us."

"I knew you didn't savvy," Wesley said. "But let me see if I can make it clear." He lowered the Kentucky. "Mountain men aren't like you or even me. They're part white, part Injun, and part animal—"

"Part animal?" Cranston laughed and slapped his leg. "Mister, I might be young but I wasn't hatched yesterday."

"When I say part animal I mean just that, boy. They've lived among the wild things so long that they become part wild themselves. This Nate King killed one of the toughest men I knew, and he did it without hardly batting an eye. So, as good as I am in the woods, I'm not taking him lightly. You'd be wise to do the same, or the coyotes and buzzards will thank you for the meal."

"You really think he's as tough as all that?" Olan asked.

"I do," Wesley confirmed. "But don't fret. Every animal and every man has a weakness. Every single one. Weaknesses a hunter can take advantage of." He motioned at the woodland. "Take deer, for instance. All a hunter has to know is when they like to come out to graze and drink, and he has them."

"This mountain man must have a weakness, then," Olan said. He sarcastically added, "But after the way you built him up, that don't seem possible."

"His weakness rides next to him during the day and sleeps next to him at night."

Olan indulged in a vicious smile. "I take it you're talking about his woman."

Wesley nodded. "Our mountain man doesn't know it yet, but that squaw of his will be his undoing."

Nate King had to hand it to Red Fox. The Pawnee was as friendly as a Shoshone and a natural-born storyteller.

Red Fox had been entertaining them with tales of the Pawnee way of life. He told about the time his people and the Crows fought a great battle and how he counted his first coup by running up to a Crow warrior and striking the Crow across the temple. "I was filled with pride that night. I thought counting coup was everything."

Nate sympathized. His son was once the same way. Zach had lived for battle, for counting the most coup of any Shoshone ever. Nate lost count of the number of times it nearly cost Zach his life. He was relieved beyond measure when Zach married and settled down.

"A man changes as he grows," Red Fox was saying. "When he is young, his blood is hot and he wants only to prove his manhood. When he is older, he sees more worth in helping others than in taking their lives. Among my people, the greatest leaders are those who think of the welfare of all."

"A wise sentiment," Winona said. "It is the same among mine."

Nate had been struck by the many beliefs different tribes shared, tribes that otherwise were always at war with one another. But whites were no better; their governments delighted in making peace treaties that they then broke to justify going to war.

"My people in the South don't have leaders," Samuel Worth commented. "Not the way you two do."

"How can you say that?" Emala took exception. "Brother Simon held services every Sunday, and Manday was an overseer."

"Overseers are picked by the whites to keep the rest of us blacks down. That's not bein' a leader.

That's takin' a whip to the backs of those who don't work hard enough to suit you."

"There's still Brother Simon."

"He was a windbag. He had no schoolin'. He just took to callin' himself Brother and carryin' around a Bible, and the next thing, folks looked up to him as the black Moses."

"The things that come out of your mouth, Samuel Worth."

Nate nipped their spat in the bud by saying, "There has been talk of freeing all the slaves one day soon. The state where I was born, New York, has already outlawed slavery."

"Many winters ago the French made slaves of some of my people," Red Fox interjected. "They were carried away and never seen again."

"Whites have made slaves of red men as well as black men?" Samuel snorted.

"And black women," Emala said.

Nate felt compelled to mention, "The Romans were white, and they had white slaves. The same with the Greeks. And in north Africa, the Arabs have made slaves of just about everybody for a thousand years or more."

"It is not right to make a slave of anyone," Red Fox said.

"I couldn't agree more," Samuel responded.

"It is better to kill an enemy than to make a slave of him," Red Fox went on. "Why put an enemy to work when that is what women are for?"

"Oh, brother," Randa said.

"Can't we talk about somethin' else?" Emala requested. "All this talk of slavery makes me miserable."

"You're the reason why not much has been done about it," Samuel told her. "Too many of our kind stick their heads in the sand."

Nate began to wonder if the pair ever got along. Since he met them, all they did was quarrel. It was to the point where if Samuel said it was hot, Emala would say it was cold.

Red Fox surprised all of them by turning to Samuel and offering, "Come live with my people. We do not have slaves. We would adopt you and you would be as one of us."

"You're joshin'," Emala said.

"I speak with a straight tongue. The Crows have a black man. They say he brings them strong medicine. If you come live with us, we will have strong medicine, too."

"If this don't beat all."

"Hush, Emala." Samuel thoughtfully regarded Red Fox. "Let me see if I understand. You want us to live as you do? In a lodge in your village? And wear animal hides? And hunt buffalo and whatnot?"

"And skin them, yes. And go on raids and lift the scalps of our enemies. Can you think of a better life?"

Nate gave Samuel a sharp look to warn him not to say anything that would antagonize the Pawnees.

"That life is fine for you and yours, but not so fine for me and mine."

"Sorry?"

"I tilled the soil back on the plantation. I didn't hunt or fish or any of that. If it wasn't for Nate and his wife, we'd have long since starved."

"Then you will come live with us?"

"Aren't you payin' attention? I thank you for the invite. I truly do. But I'd make a terrible Indian." Samuel shook his head. "We're bound for King Valley. I can't wait to get there. To hear Nate describe it, it's heaven on earth."

Nate hadn't made any such claim. He was about to set them straight when a feeling came over him, a feeling that they were being watched. Shifting, he stared beyond the ring of firelight into the dark. It could be anything, he told himself. A bear. Deer. A coyote or a wolf. Or just his imagination.

"Is something wrong, Grizzly Killer?" Red Fox asked.

"For a second there I thought—" Nate caught himself. He didn't want to come across as silly. "It's nothing."

The Pawnee children were soon made to turn in, and their mothers shortly followed. The Worths started yawning about ten, and Emala excused herself and her offspring. That left the men and Winona. Red Fox stayed up late, plying them with questions about the Shoshones and other tribes and translating for his friend, whose name was Hawk Takes Wing.

It was pushing midnight by Nate's figuring when Winona announced her eyelids were too heavy for her to stay awake. Samuel turned in after her, and then the two warriors.

That left Nate. He refilled his tin cup with piping hot coffee and sat back. He had agreed to keep watch until three, and then he would wake Winona. As he raised the cup to his lips, that feeling came over him again. The feeling that he was being watched. Puzzled, he gazed about the clearing. All was peaceful.

He hoped it stayed that way.

Chapter Five

The Kings and the Worths rode out the next morning an hour after the sun came up. Usually they were under way at the crack of dawn, but Nate let the others sleep in. They could use the extra rest. More important, so could their mounts. It was a long way from the Mississippi River to the Rocky Mountains—weeks and weeks of travel that took a toll on rider and mount.

The Pawnees were up early. They went about their chores quietly. The children gathered wood and the women got a fire going. Red Fox and Hawk Takes Wing were preparing to ride out in search of buffalo.

"One more kill and we will head back to our village," Red Fox mentioned. "Our pack animals cannot carry much more meat."

"I wish you success in your hunt," Nate said sincerely, and offered his hand in the white fashion.

Red Fox stared at it, then smiled and shook. "I am proud to call Grizzly Killer my friend."

"Perhaps one day our two families can get together again."

"I would like that."

Nate was almost sorry to ride off. He would have enjoyed more of Red Fox's company. But he was eager to reach the valley he now called home and make sure his son, Zach, and his best friend, Shake-speare McNair, hadn't gotten into any trouble in his absence. McNair knew better, as old as he was. But Zach was young and rash, and often as not got into hot water without half trying.

Strung out single file, they pushed on. They had been under way only a short while when Nate, who was in the lead, was joined by someone else.

"They sure were nice Injuns," Emala Worth said.

"You sound surprised."

"I don't mind admittin' I am. I mean, your wife is as sweet a woman as ever I met, and I adore her. But I never figured on liking other Injuns as much as I like that there Red Fox."

"You're learning."

"I am? What, exactly?"

"That it doesn't matter what color skin a person has. People are people. There are good ones and bad ones of every color. The thing is to savvy enough to tell the difference."

"You're awful smart for a man who lives up in the Rocky Mountains," Emala said.

Nate chuckled. "Anyone who likes the wilderness must be stupid?"

"No, no, I didn't mean that at all. You're sure not. You speak as well as Master Justin and Master Frederick ever did. Must come from you bein' a reader and all."

"I suppose that has something to do with it."

"Your wife is awful smart, too. She knows more languages than I have fingers. And she says your son and your girl are the same as the two of you."

"Nate realized she was trying to make a point. "What are you trying to tell me, Emala?"

"Just this: I don't want to impose. But I've been thinkin' and I've got a favor to ask."

"You want us to watch Randa and Chickory so you and your husband can go off by yourselves this evening?"

Emala blinked, then snorted, then burst into hearty laughter. "Oh, Mr. King. You are a dreadful tease. Samuel and me haven't fooled around since we went on the run, and I don't know as I will again until I have a roof over my head."

"Then what's the favor?"

"I'd like to ask if you and your missus would mind teachin' my girl and my boy learnin'."

"How much schooling have they had?"

"None."

Nate nearly drew rein. "None whatsoever?"

"We were slaves, Mr. King. The folks who owned us didn't allow for no schoolin'. All they cared about was that we tended their cotton fields and did the other work they made us do." Emala sighed. "I can read, thanks to my ma. She taught me her own self. I tried to teach mine, but they didn't take to it like I did."

"And your husband?"

"Samuel can't read or write a lick. I offered to teach him to read, but he couldn't be bothered. Said it wouldn't do him no good."

"Learning to read opens up whole new worlds," Nate said. He was thinking of the works of Irving and Cooper and the poetry of Byron that he had on his bookshelf in his cabin.

"Our owners didn't want us openin' new worlds. They wanted us to be content with what we had."

Nate tried to imagine what it must have been like

to be lorded over by others, to have no say in one's own life, to be treated as property instead of as people. "I feel sorry for you, Emala."

"Goodness. I'm grateful you care, but I don't want your pity. I doubt Samuel does, either."

"You've lived a hard life."

"So? Except for the rich, who doesn't? I'm not complain', mind you. I won't shed tears over who I am or where I was born. I had no say in that and it does no good to whine over things that are."

"I agree."

"But now I can do as I please, and it pleases me to try to better my children. What do you say? Will you do it?"

"I'm not sure exactly what you want us to teach."

"Readin' and writin'. Randa can read a little, but she's never read an entire book in her life. As for Chickory, he takes after his father. Which is too bad. The last thing this world needs is two Samuel Worths."

"You're awful hard on him."

"Oh, please. He's a grown man. He can take it. Besides, ask any woman and she will tell you that men are like bulls. They're ornery and stubborn and have to be led around by the nose or they get into all sorts of trouble."

"Oh, Emala . . ."

"What? As God is my witness, I'm speakin' the truth. But what do you say? Will you help us? Can you teach my kids to talk as good as your wife and read like you do?"

"Wait. You think my wife talks better than I do?"

"Oh, Lord, yes. Winona is a wonderment. She is as red as I am black, yet she speaks white better than both of us."

Nate wasn't being told anything he didn't already know. "I sure married a smart lady."

"That you did. Me, I married a man with more stubborn between his ears than brains."

"Oh, Emala . . ."

"Why do you keep sayin' that? If I speak my mind, it's because I have a lot of mind to speak and I'm not shy about speakin' it."

"I'm going to like having you for a neighbor."

"Really?"

"Just remember, if Samuel and you ever need us to watch your kids for a night so you two can be frisky, let us know."

"Oh, Mr. King . . ."

Red Fox was pleased. He and Hawk Takes Wing found a small herd of buffalo early in the day and brought one down, and now they were headed back to their camp on the Platte River to get their wives. Pawnee men did the hunting; the women did the skinning and the butchering. That was how it had always been for as long as any Pawnee could remember.

The sun shone bright in a pale blue sky. Around them, the grass was stirred by a welcome breeze.

Red Fox loved the prairie. The unending green, the splashes of flower color, the many kinds of animals, were a spectacle of which he never tired. The mountains, with their thick forests and deep canyons, were nice, but he loved the prairie more.

On this particular morning, Hawk Takes Wing was in fine spirits, too. "Once the women have cut and dried the meat we can return to our village."

Red Fox grunted. He was looking forward to that. As much as he loved to hunt, he loved his people more. It gave him great satisfaction to fill their bellies.

Unexpectedly, Hawk Takes Wing asked, "What did you think of Grizzly Killer?"

"If more whites were like him, I would respect whites more."

"Do you think he has killed as many of the great bears as they say he has? I heard he has killed fifty, but that cannot be."

"I asked him. He said he does not remember the exact number. For a white man he is humble."

"That surprised me. Many whites strut around like elk in rut. Even when they are rabbits."

Red Fox chuckled. "I can see why the Shoshones adopted him. I hope I see him again."

"I liked his black friends. Their skin is like the night. And did you see their hair? A black scalp would be powerful medicine."

"Grizzly Killer told me there are many blacks where those came from. More blacks than there are Pawnees."

"Do you believe him?"

"If I am any judge of men, Grizzly Killer always speaks with a straight tongue." Red Fox gazed thoughtfully to the east. "And if he does, then the day will come when our people must make an important decision."

"Explain."

"Grizzly Killer says there are more of his own people than there are blades of grass. He says they are as numberless as the stars at night. He says that they have taken up all the land east of the father of rivers and that there will come a day when they push west of it and take up all this land, too."

Hawk Takes Wing laughed. "Perhaps he boasts.

There cannot be that many whites. Why, that would mean there are more of them than there are buffalo."

"It troubles me," Red Fox said.

"Fagh! Even if he does speak true, that day is many winters away. You and I will not live to see it."

"I hope you are right."

In the distance, the belt of trees and undergrowth that fringed the Platte River lined the horizon. The river itself was visible as patches of blue amid the boles.

As they drew near, Hawk Takes Wing remarked, "I see smoke."

Red Fox straightened. So did he. And there shouldn't have been. The women knew not to give away their presence by being careless. Smoke could bring enemies; the Sioux or the Blackfeet would delight in counting coup on Pawnees.

"We must scold them for this," Hawk Takes Wing said, and jabbed his heels against his horse.

Red Fox made no effort to catch up. He would let his friend handle it. Hawk Takes Wing would be harder on the women than he would. He was content to ride at a leisurely pace and enjoy the splendor of the prairie. He saw Hawk Takes Wing gallop in among the trees, and then there was a commotion of some kind. Out raced Hawk Takes Wing's sorrel, only without a rider. Thinking his friend had dismounted and something must have spooked the horse, Red Fox flicked his reins and rode to cut it off. Fortunately it stopped and didn't shy when he came up and grabbed the rope reins to lead it back.

The strip of woodland was quiet. Somewhere a robin sang. Sparrows flitted about.

Red Fox came to the clearing and for a few moments could not make sense of what he was seeing.

Everyone seemed to be asleep. The women and children were sprawled on their backs and their bellies. Even Hawk Takes Wing had lain down. Then Red Fox saw the blood. Shock slowed him as he raised his hand to his quiver. He didn't quite have an arrow out when men rushed from both sides. Hands seized him and threw him to the ground. He lost his bow. He tried for his knife, but his attackers had hold of his arms, and the next instant he was roughly hauled to his feet. He struggled, but they were too strong.

"Behave and you'll live a little longer, redskin."

The speaker was a tall white in buckskins, a fine rifle cradled in the crook of an elbow.

Red Fox stood still, his chin jutting in defiance. Inwardly, he struggled to contain his grief and his rage.

"He understood you, Wesley," said a bear of a man with a great beard. "He must speak English."

"Is that true, redskin? Do you savvy the white tongue?"

Red Fox had to clear his throat. "I speak it well."

"Will wonders never cease," a short man said.

The one called Wesley placed the stock of his rifle on the ground and leaned on the barrel. "Listen, redskin. We're after Nate King and the darkies he's helping. If you speak English, like as not you and him had some long talks. Did he say where he's headed? Will he stop at Bent's Fort on his way up into the mountains? I doubt he'll live to reach it but you never know."

"I will not tell you."

"That's where you're wrong." Wesley drew a hunting knife and wagged it so that the blade glinted in the sunlight. "I'm in no hurry. I'll carve on you all day if that's what it takes. And in the end, you'll tell me. You'll tell me everything. They always do."

Red Fox gazed at his dead wife and their dead children, and his sorrow was boundless. From it he drew strength. He refused to show weakness.

"Say something," Wesley said. "Show me you're not as stupid as most of your kind."

"I have had a good life," Red Fox said.

"Well, bully for you," mocked a man with a bristly mustache.

"I have one regret."

The man called Wesley tilted his head. "What would that be, redskin?"

"That I will not live to see Grizzly Killer kill you."

Chapter Six

Nate King was enjoying himself. He was enjoying himself too much.

If there was one lesson Nate had learned during his years on the frontier, it was that only the alert and the quick and the strong survived. The evidence was all around him. In the natural world, the unwary fell to the meat eaters. The slow fell to the fast. The weak fell to the strong.

Predator-and-prey was the order of things. The elk past its prime was pulled down by wolves. The careless doe was pounced on by a mountain lion. The rabbit that didn't jump at shadows was impaled by the talons of the hawk.

The same held true when predators clashed. When two bears fought, inevitably the strongest won. When bull buffalo bumped heads, invariably the strongest head beat down the weaker.

It was a lesson Nate learned the hard way. Too many times to count, he let down his guard and paid for his mistake with his blood or a narrow escape from the grave. He learned to *always* be alert, no matter where or when.

So it was that as his party wound along the Platte River toward the far off Rockies, Nate grew upset with himself. He liked the Worths; he liked them a lot. Samuel was a good companion. Emala made him laugh. Randa and Chickory were endless founts of curiosity. The trouble was, he liked them too much. He was paying attention to them and not to their surroundings.

On this particular day, with the blazing sun high in the afternoon sky, Nate mopped his brow with his sleeve and remarked to his sager half, "We need to be more watchful."

Winona was admiring the antics of a goldfinch and its mate. "Have you seen sign I've missed?"

"No, only animal tracks. But we're close to Sioux country."

"Strange you should mention it, Husband."

"Why?"

"It is probably nothing. But I have been uneasy for a while now. Nerves, I suppose."

"You have the calmest disposition of anyone I've ever known," Nate said, praising her.

"Thank you. But that is not true. Blue Water Woman never lets anything fluster her. I often wish I were more like she is."

Nate grunted. Blue Water Woman was the Flathead wife of his best friend, Shakespeare McNair. "Why haven't you said something?"

Winona shrugged. "I thought I was being silly. I wake up at night thinking something is wrong, but everything is fine. I feel I am being watched, but I never am."

"Damn."

"I do wish you would stop saying that. You never swore when you were younger. It is a habit you can do without."

Nate remembered the language used by his fellow trappers at the rendezvous, back in the days when beaver plews were worth good money. "You're starting to sound like Emala," he teased.

"She is a good woman. We will be fast friends."

Nate raised his reins. "This unease of yours . . . Maybe I should take a look around."

"Now?"

"It will be hours yet until sundown. There's plenty of time." Nate touched her arm, then wheeled his bay and rode back along the line, passing each of the Worths.

Randa was last, and she brightened as he approached. "What are you up to, Mr. King? If you don't mind my askin'."

"I keep asking you to call me by my first name."

"Sorry. My ma raised me to always be polite."

Nate nodded at the woodland behind them. "I'm going to check our back trail."

"Can I come along?"

Nate knew Winona would tease him no end. But he gave a different reason. "There's no telling what or who I'll run into. I have to do it alone."

"Be careful. Please."

"Always." Nate brought the bay to a trot until he was out of her sight, then slowed to a walk again. To his left gurgled the Platte. The river consisted mainly of long sandy channels fringed with vegetation. Here and there were deeper pools.

Presently he emerged from heavy growth into an open area with wetlands on either side. A pair of cranes took flight, their necks almost as long as their legs. A harmless ribbon snake slithered from his path. To the south a hawk soared on the air currents.

Nate breathed deep and smiled. God, how he loved the wilderness! He never tired of the splendor, never wearied of the parade of life. He shuddered to think that once he wanted to be an accountant. He would have spent his entire life in a dimly lit office, scribbling in ledgers. No sun, no wind in his hair, no dank earth under his feet. Just him and the office and his reflection in a mirror. "Thank you, Lord," he said out loud.

Another crane took wing. The flapping drew Nate out of himself and back to the here and now. Once again he had let himself be distracted. He was falling into a number of bad habits of late. Shaking his head to clear it, he focused on his surroundings. "The last thing I need is an arrow in the back."

Nate chuckled. Talking to himself was another habit he could do without. Patting the bay, he said, "I'm downright pitiful."

More than a mile more of riding brought him to a bank choked by heavy thickets. Rather than inflict the briars on the bay, Nate reined to the right to go around. He gazed out over the prairie and spied several specks on the horizon. Buffalo, if he was any judge, maybe stragglers from a herd that had passed through. He was tempted to try to get closer. Buffalo meat was just about his favorite, second only to mountain lion. But without a packhorse he wouldn't be able to bring much of the meat back, and he hated to think of nearly an entire buff going to waste.

Nate faced front and stiffened.

Up ahead was a rider, a frontiersman in greasy buckskins. The man had drawn rein and a friendly smile creased his salt-and-pepper beard. He had a rifle, but the stock was on his thigh and the muzzle pointed at the sky.

Nate scanned the vicinity but saw no one else. Leveling the Hawken, he slowly approached.

"I mean no harm, friend. Truly, I don't," the stranger said.

"A man can never be too careful," Nate responded. He was trying to place the face; it was not anyone he'd ever met.

"That we can't." The rider's smile widened. "I'm Peleg Harrod."

"Peleg?"

"My ma lived and breathed her Bible. She named all ten of us by opening to a page and picking the first name she saw. I was one of the lucky ones. I've got a brother called Mizzah and another called Zelophehad." Harrod laughed. "Then there are my sisters. One was named Timna, after a concubine. Another is Ahinoam."

Nate introduced himself.

"King, you say? Why does that name strike a chord? You're not by any chance the same King who is a good friend of Shakespeare McNair's?"

"You know McNair?"

"I've heard of him," Harrod said. "But then, who hasn't? He's older than Methuselah, or so they say. One of the first whites to ever set foot in the Rockies. I reckon he's as famous as Bridger, Walker and Carson put together."

"Don't tell him that or his head will swell up even bigger than it already is," Nate mentioned. Not that McNair thought too highly of himself; quite the contrary.

Harrod liked to laugh. "Well, fancy this. Meeting someone like you way out here." He bobbed his bearded chin. "I'm heading for the mountains. Can't wait to get there. I just spent a few weeks back east and I'm hankering to set eyes on the high country."

"We're bound for there too."

"We?"

Nate mentally kicked himself. Harrod seemed friendly enough, but a person could never be too careful. "I'm with some others."

"You don't say? I'm by my lonesome, but I wouldn't mind company. That is, if you don't object."

"I suppose not." Nate gazed past Harrod, but there was no sign of anyone else. It was rare to come across someone alone on the prairie, but then, he'd crossed it a few times by himself.

Nate reined around and beckoned. "Ride with me and we'll jaw." Better that the stranger was beside him than behind him.

Harrod came up next to him. "I'm obliged."

"You haven't come across any sign of hostiles, have you?"

"Sure haven't. And I don't care to. I'm powerful fond of what hair I have left."

"That's good to hear. I was worried Sioux might be in the area."

"Let's hope not. They're tricky devils and they don't care a lick for whites. You'd think they were Blackfeet, they like counting coup on whites so much."

"You know your Indians."

"So do you, I hear. Is it true you were adopted by the Shoshones?"

Nate hadn't realized that was common knowledge. "Some years ago, yes. My wife is Shoshone."

"Well now. That must have been quite some honor. Me, I've always been too skittish about having my hair lifted to take up with redskins." Harrod quickly added, "No offense meant."

"None taken."

Harrod showed more teeth. "I wouldn't want us to get off on the wrong foot."

They rode in silence for a while, until Nate shifted in the saddle to glance behind them.

"So, tell me, are you returning from a visit back east, too?" asked Harrod.

"I had to have my Hawken repaired."

"Ah. You took it to the Hawken brothers? Smart thinking. Other gunsmiths do fine work, but no one can match Jacob and Samuel."

Nate felt the same. They were the best. He would no more take his rifle to someone else for repair than he would wear buckskins made by someone other than Winona.

"And to think we owe it all to two people dying," Harrod went on in his friendly fashion.

"How's that?"

"Didn't you know? Jacob and Samuel didn't start out as partners. Jacob was working with a gent named Lakenan. Samuel had his own shop. Then Samuel's wife died and he moved to St. Louis, some say to get away from the sad memories. Shortly after, that Lakenan fellow died and Jacob went to St. Louis to be with Samuel."

"You know more about them than I do."

Harrod chuckled. "When you've lived as long as I have, you pick up kernels here and there. For instance, I've heard that your friend Shakespeare McNair has a Flathead wife. And I've heard it said that your son is a regular hellion and best fought shy of."

"You sure hear a lot. My son's been in a few scrapes, yes."

"Say no more. I was young once. Had me a temper you wouldn't believe. And not much common sense, either. Or I likely wouldn't have struck off for the mountains to trap beaver for a living. Not when I didn't know a thing about the mountains and even less about beaver."

Nate found himself warming to the older man. Harrod was a talker, that was for sure. It reminded him of his mentor, McNair. "I was the same way."

"Do tell. I reckon a lot of us didn't have the brains of tree stumps. How else to explain why we put our lives at risk for the privilege of setting traps in ice-cold streams and risk having hostiles hang our hair on their coup sticks." Harrod chuckled. "I thought I knew it all."

"The young never learn how fragile they are."

Harrod glanced sharply at him. "Why, that's almost poetical, that is. No one ever told me you have such a way with words."

Nate shrugged. "I read a lot."

"Is that a fact? I never got beyond the second grade. My ma wanted me to stick it out to the sixth, but I was always acting up and the teacher didn't take kindly to my antics. He didn't take kindly to them at all. Must have rapped my knuckles ten times a day with that ruler of his."

"My father wouldn't have let me quit school even if I'd wanted to."

"One of those, was he? My pa lit out on us when I was four. Never did learn why. Ma said he took up with another woman but a friend of his told me he couldn't take ma's nagging anymore. Seems to me, though, that if a man says 'I do,' he shouldn't abandon a gal just because she's fond of flapping her gums."

Now it was Nate who grinned. "You have a way

with words yourself. Well put. Of all the virtues, I value loyalty pretty near the most."

"Virtues, huh?" Harrod snickered. "I won't lie to you and claim more than my share. I have my weaknesses, I am afraid. Money is one of them."

"Oh?"

"Money is what brought me to the mountains to trap. Remember all the talk back then? About how a coon could make a small fortune for a few measly months of work?"

"It wasn't entirely a lie," Nate said. The best trappers earned upward of two thousand dollars at the rendezvous, at a time when most men back east were lucky to make three hundred dollars a year.

"Maybe so. But if I told you some of the other things I've done for money, you'd laugh. I'd laugh too except that some of my harebrained notions have cost me in scars and skin."

"You're not the only one."

Harrod didn't seem to hear him. "I'm just letting you know I'm no angel, so you don't hold it against me later if I prove to be less than perfect."

"Don't worry," Nate said. "I won't hold you to a higher standard than I'd hold anyone else. So long as you show some common courtesy, you're welcome to ride with us for as long as you like."

Peleg Harrod beamed. "You don't know how happy I am to hear you say that."

Chapter Seven

Everyone took to the new member of their little party. At first the Worths held back, but after several days and nights of the old frontiersman's smiles and chatter, they were won over. Randa, in particular, loved to hear his stories about all he had done and seen in his travels.

Everyone took to the new member—except for Winona King. She couldn't say what it was about Harrod, but something about him bothered her. She kept it to herself, thinking it silly, until the morning of the fourth day. She was up before first light. Chickory was supposed to be keeping watch. They all took turns. But the boy had dozed off and let the fire go out.

Winona quietly rose from under the blankets so as not to awaken her husband. She stretched, then walked toward the charred embers, smoothing her dress. She didn't look up until she was almost there.

Peleg Harrod was missing.

Winona gazed about the clearing. Everyone else was still asleep. But Harrod's blankets were thrown back, and he was gone. She figured he had risen and gone off to wash up in the Platte. Kneeling, she set to rekindling the fire. Chickory let out a snore, and she grinned. Over the past weeks she had grown quite fond of the Worths. It had been her idea to have Nate ask them if they would like to settle in King Valley. Nate had proven reluctant, and she had probed to find out why.

"What is wrong, Husband? You do not want them to live near us because they are black?"

Nate had stiffened in indignation. "If I were that way, would I have married you?"

"I am red, or so your people say, and not black."

"Don't quibble. If you honestly and truly think that I judge people by the color of their skin, say so now and I'll go off and live by myself."

Winona had arched an eyebrow. "You are making more of this than it deserves."

"Not when you just called me a bigot, I'm not."

"Never in a million winters would I think that," Winona had assured him. Placing her hand on his broad chest, she had smiled up into his troubled eyes. "I love you more than I love life. I am sorry if I have hurt your feelings."

"That's better."

"So tell me why you do not want them to come to our valley? What reason could you have? It is not as if we want for space. There are three cabins and a lodge in a valley that is"—Winona had paused, trying to remember what he told her once—"big enough for a thousand families."

"One more might not seem like a lot to you," Nate had responded, "but when we first moved there, the idea was to get off by ourselves. We were too near the Oregon Trail, where we lived before. Too near the foothills."

"I remember." It had seemed to Winona as if strangers happened by every time she turned around.

"It was supposed to be only us and Zach and Lou and Shakespeare and Blue Water Woman. Then the Nansusequas showed up and you were too kind-hearted to turn them away."

"That was your decision, not mine," Winona corrected. "You are the one with the kind heart, although you try to hide that you have one."

Nate ignored her comment. "Now you've invited the Worths. At the rate we're going, we'll have us our very own city in no time."

"Oh, Husband." Winona had laughed heartily. "I understand, though. We will let the Worths stay, but no one else after them. Agreed?"

Nate had nodded and the matter was settled.

Now, as Winona poked a stick at the embers and thin wisps of smoke rose into the crisp morning air, she thought of how surprised her son and their friends the Nansusequas would be. New settlers were one thing; blacks were quite another. The Worths were so unlike her people and the whites, and yet so much like them, too. She looked forward to many a day spent in Emala's company, learning all there was to learn about her kind.

One of the horses nickered, and Winona glanced up.

Harrod was coming back but not from the direction of the river. He was coming from the east, which struck Winona as strange. He saw her at the same instant she saw him, and he stopped short as if in surprise. Then, wearing his perpetual smile, he strolled into the clearing.

"Good morning, Mrs. King. You're up awful early this fine morning. The sun hasn't risen yet."

"The same could be said of you."

"Oh, I've always been an early riser," Harrod said.

"I was raised on a farm, and we had to be up and out at the crack of dawn to milk the cows and collect chicken eggs and such."

Bending to puff on a red ember, Winona asked, "See anything on your walk?"

"Just the usual. A few deer. A few birds." Harrod coughed. "Why do you ask?"

"No reason." When the flames were high enough to suit her, Winona picked up the coffeepot and shook it. "Empty. I need to make more. My husband is unable to start his day without a cup or two."

"I'm the same way." Harrod cradled his rifle. "How about if I walk with you? Just in case."

"In case what?"

"In case a griz happens by. Or a cougar. Or a pack of wolves." Harrod grinned. "Then there are the two-legged kind who wear paint and like to lift hair."

"I have these," Winona said, patting the flintlocks tucked under the leather belt she wore. "But you may come with me if you wish." She went and got her own rifle.

"You sure are a cautious soul."

"I take that as a compliment, Mr. Harrod. My husband likes to say that the more cautious we are, the longer we live."

"Smart gent, that man of yours."

"I have always thought so, yes."

They were passing through a stand of cottonwoods, the trunks pale in the predawn light. Here and there were a few willows and oaks.

Winona breathed deep and admired the pink tinge on the eastern horizon.

"May I ask you a question, Mrs. King?"

"So long as it is not personal."

"I was just wondering how it is that you chose to

live with a white man when you likely could have had your pick of any buck in your tribe?"

Winona stopped and looked at him. "In the first place, I said no personal questions. But for your information, I married my husband because I love him. In the second place, I will thank you not to call the men of my tribe 'bucks.'"

"What's wrong? Whites do it all the time."

"It is like calling me a squaw."

Harrod shrugged, then smiled. "If I stepped over the line, I'm right sorry. I always aim to please."

Winona walked on. Once again that feeling of distrust came over her. But other than ask a question he had no business asking, he had done nothing wrong. His next comment startled her.

"You don't like me very much."

"What gives you that idea?"

"It's hard to put into words. Let's say I feel it in my bones. But I don't see why. I've always held females in high respect. Even red ones."

"What is that white saying? Oh, yes. You keep putting your foot in your mouth."

Harrod scratched his chin and studied her, more amused than offended. "The last thing I want is to have you upset with me. I'm grateful to your husband for letting me tag along. It gets lonesome crossing the prairie alone."

Winona said nothing. She was amazed he had sensed her feelings. She wondered whether she had given them away somehow.

"It's safer for me, traveling with you. I don't mind admitting that's one of the reasons I asked. But if you're against it for some reason, say so now and I'll go my own way."

For one of the few times in her life, Winona went

against her better judgment. "Where you got these notions from, I will never know. My husband invited you, so you are welcome to ride with us for as long as you like."

"Thank you, ma'am. You're about the sweetest gal I've ever come across, and I mean that sincerely."

"Be careful not to overdo it."

Harrod laughed. "Don't you beat all. But don't worry, I'll try not to praise you if I can help it."

The trees thinned and the ribbon of blue that was the Platte spread before them. Winona moved down the bank and knelt. She removed the top of the coffeepot and dipped the pot in the river. The water was pleasantly cool. She noticed the old frontiersman studying her again. "What?"

"I was just wondering."

"About?"

"I'd better not. You'll be even more upset with me."

"Not if I can help it," Winona assured him. She looked downriver and then upriver, and thought she saw movement in trees a half mile away. A hint of brown. Deer, she guessed.

"Since you insist, I'm curious: How come you and your husband have taken up with the Worths?"

"They are nice people."

"That's not what I meant. They're black. Doesn't that bother you any?"

"Should it?"

"Heavens, no. It's just that I know a few folks it would bother. Some men who hate blacks just because they *are* black. Men who would put a slug between their eyes for no reason other than they think the world would be a better place without them."

The irony of his words was not lost on Winona. Here she was being asked the very thing she had asked Nate. "I take people as they are. I judge them by how they act, not by their skin."

"That's mighty noble of you," Harrod said, "but a lot of people don't share your high ideals. Me, I'm the same as you. I take everyone pretty much as they are."

Winona couldn't let his bald-faced lie pass. "Yet you never forget their color, do you?" If her goal was to fluster him, it worked

"No, I don't, and I'll tell you why. People ain't the same. I don't care what anybody says, whites don't act like blacks and blacks don't act like whites and neither whites nor blacks act and think like the red."

"We have more in common than you think." Winona raised the pot out of the river. Water sloshed over the rim and splashed on her dress.

"Can you give me a for instance?"

"We have hearts, Mr. Harrod. Red people have hearts and white people have hearts and black people have hearts. And in those hearts are the same yearnings for happiness and love. *That* is what we have in common."

"You don't really believe that?"

"I would not say it if it were not true." Wheeling, Winona headed back. He quickly caught up.

"Dang. You talk like no female I ever come across. Like no male, either. Where do you get these highfalutin notions? From your husband?"

"I get them from life, Mr. Harrod. Do you know that among my people, the Shoshones, there is one trait held in higher esteem than any other? Can you guess what that trait is?"

"Esteem, you say? That's where you think highly of something or other, right? If I was to guess, I'd say that for Shoshone warriors, counting coup counts more than anything else."

"We are bloodthirsty savages, is that it?" Winona sighed sadly. "No, Mr. Harrod. The trait my people admire most is wisdom."

"You're pulling my leg."

"I would never touch so much as your toe, Mr. Harrod."

"But wisdom? What does that mean, exactly? What *is* wisdom? Is your wisdom the same as mine or anybody else's?"

"Among my people, a wise leader is one who looks out for their welfare. A wise warrior is one who knows when to count coup and when not to count coup. A wise woman is one who keeps her lodge in order and imparts to her children the things they must know to live a long, happy life."

"How you talk . . ." Harrod marveled. "You make flowers of words."

"It is your tongue, Mr. Harrod. Why whites do not learn it better has always puzzled me."

"You sure are something," the frontiersman went on. "No wonder your husband is so powerful fond of you. Too bad I didn't meet you before he did. You might be mine instead of his."

"That would never be."

"Why not?"

"You are not him."

Nate was up, adjusting his powder horn and ammo pouch across his chest. "There you two are. I wondered where you got to."

"This wife of yours is a wonderment," Harrod said. "If more females were like her, there'd be less for us men to grumble about."

"You get no argument from me."

Harrod nodded at him and smiled at Winona and walked off whistling, as happy as could be.

"Nice man," Nate remarked.

"He is full of flattery," Winona said. "In the past ten minutes he has praised me more than you do in a year."

"That just shows how nice he is."

"No, Husband. It shows we must not trust him any farther than you can throw a buffalo."

Chapter Eight

Chickory Worth lost sight of the buck he had been following and frowned. He had been gone from camp too long. His parents would worry. They'd likely ask Nate King to come find him, which would embarrass him something awful. It was sometimes hard being the youngest.

Chickory was fourteen, three years younger than Randa, but it was the difference between being treated like a man and being treated like a child. Randa, his parents thought of as a grown woman, but him, he might as well have been ten. It upset him no end.

Chickory was trying his best to show how mature he could be. He helped with camp chores. He took a turn standing watch at night. He never complained. But one thing he hadn't done, and would very much like to do, was to contribute to the supper pot. Nate and Winona shot game all the time. The newcomer, Harrod, had brought down a buck and a grouse in the few days he had been with them. His own pa shot a rabbit once.

So it was that when they had stopped at noon to rest the horses, Chickory went over to where his father was sitting. He was careful to make sure his mother was busy with Winona King before he quietly said, "I have somethin' to ask you, Pa."

"Ask away."

"Do you suppose you could lend me that pistol Mr. King bought for you back in Missouri?"

His father had glanced up. "What on earth do you want that for? And don't you remember your mother sayin' you weren't to touch it no matter what?"

"I remember," Chickory admitted. "But she doesn't understand things like you do."

"False praise is no praise, Son. Suppose you come right out with it and let me be the judge."

Afraid the answer would be no, Chickory poked at the ground with his toe. "All right. I want to do some huntin' while everyone is restin'. I won't be long. I promise."

"Huntin'?" Samual repeated.

"Yes, sir. For somethin' to eat. I want to show Mr. King I can do my share."

"Help with the horses. Tote water. Those sorts of things. Leave the huntin' for them as is hunters."

"Please, Pa. I never ask you for much, do I? But I'd sure like the chance. It'd mean a lot to me."

"You ain't never fired a gun before but once," Samuel reminded him.

"But I remember how it's done." Chickory had put a hand on his father's shoulder. "Please, Pa."

"Damnation." Samuel had looked toward Emala and lowered his voice. "If your ma hears of this, she'll take the gun from you and use it to club me to death."

"I won't say a word. I promise. I'll sneak off and sneak back and she'll never know."

"How are you goin' to sneak back with a dead animal over your horse?"

"Please."

Now here Chickory was, riding parallel with the Platte, the heavy flintlock in his hand, his thumb on the hammer. He needed to get close. Pistols didn't shoot as far as rifles. Even he knew that. "Where did you get to?" he wondered under his breath.

Some sparrows took wing, chirping merrily, and Chickory watched them in amusement. He loved the wild, loved all the creatures, the birds and the butterflies and the many other kinds of animals.

Most of all, Chickory loved being free. He never liked being a slave, never liked it at all. To be owned by someone else, to have to answer to their every whim, to work from dawn till dusk and have nothing to show for it but calluses and scrapes—that wasn't the life for him. He was all for running when his pa brought it up.

Better to run free than to die as property.

Chickory couldn't wait to reach the valley the Kings had told them about. They'd have their own cabin. They could hunt and fish and plant crops; Winona said she had seeds they could have. They could do whatever they wanted with no one to tell them different.

That was the glory of being free.

Chickory had long imagined how wonderful it would be. But it was even better. To have the right to decide for himself what he should do with each day, instead of being told what to do. To be his own— what was it his pa called it?—his own lord and master. There was nothing finer.

Suddenly movement under the trees caught Chickory's eye. The buck had stopped and was staring at him. He raised the pistol and squeezed the trigger but nothing happened; he'd forgotten to pull back the hammer. Quickly, he remedied his mistake, but when he went to take aim, the buck had moved into a stand of cottonwoods, and he didn't have a clear shot.

Chickory jabbed his heels against his horse. He would give himself five more minutes. If he didn't shoot the buck by then, he'd turn around and head back. Anxiously, he scanned the cottonwoods. The buck had somehow disappeared.

"Where did you get to, you tricky critter?"

Chickory reined to the right to go around the cottonwoods, thinking he could beat the buck to the other side. Intent on spotting it, he didn't realize he was no longer alone until someone laughed.

"Blind as a bat, ain't he?"

Startled, Chickory drew rein. Fear clutched at him as he laid eyes on six riders who had appeared out of nowhere. He recognized one of them—the lean, hawk-faced man in buckskins, holding a Kentucky rifle.

"You!"

"Me," the man said.

"You're that slave hunter," Chickory blurted. "The one they call . . ."—he strained to remember— "the one they call Wesley."

"Good memory, darkie."

"You're after my family and me." Chickory went to raise the flintlock but a whole bunch of metallic clicks changed his mind. The other five were pointing rifles at him.

"Don't try it, boy," said a short man whose dark eyes glittered with the threat of violence.

Wesley brought his mount up next to Chickory's and held out his hand. "The pistol."

Chickory hesitated.

"The pistol, or die."

Emala wrung her pudgy hands and paced. She gazed anxiously back the way they had come and declared, "You shouldn't have let him go."

"He wanted to help out," Samuel said.

"And you for certain shouldn't have given him that gun. He's just a slip of a boy. What on earth were you thinkin'?"

"In case you ain't noticed, he's pretty near a man. He has to learn to hunt anyway, and it might as well be now as later."

"What you know about huntin' wouldn't fill a thimble."

"Careful, woman," Samuel said. "You're much too free with insults these days."

"Can you blame me, with the strain I've been under?" Emala felt her eyes moisten. "The trials I've endured. The tribulations you've brought down on our heads."

"Me?"

"You're the one who took it on himself to make runaways of us. You're the one who hit Master Brent."

"Would you rather he raped our daughter?"

"Don't change the subject. We're talkin' about you." Emala gnawed on her lip. "Oh, Lordy. What will we do?"

From behind them came a kindly voice. "Perhaps I can help. What has you so upset?"

"Mrs. King!"

Winona had overheard a few of their remarks and divined from Emala's expression that something was wrong.

"We've imposed on you enough as it is," Emala said. "Since my Samuel was the one who let him leave, he should be the one who goes after him."

"Him?" Winona counted heads and horses. "Your son is not back from his ride yet?"

"It wasn't so much a ride as a hunt," Samuel said. "I told him we were only stoppin' for an hour or so, and he promised me he'd be back in plenty of time."

"Only he's not here," Emala said accusingly.

Samuel turned toward the horses. "But you're right. It's my doin'. I'll go after him. If we're not back before Mr. King returns, go on without us and we'll catch up."

Winona walked up to them. "My husband took Mr. Harrod and went to scout ahead. One can never be too careful near Sioux country."

"Oh, Lordy. What if they got my Chickory?"

"You three wait here. I'll go find him," Winona offered.

Samuel shook his head. "I'm his pa. It's mine to do."

"Begging your pardon," Winona said politely, "but it needs to be done quickly. I am a better rider and I have more experience at tracking." She also knew the landmarks and the wildlife, but she didn't bring that up.

Emala nodded vigorously. "Let her go, Samuel. She'll find Chickory and be back in half the time it would take you."

Winona hurried to her mare, swung on, and reined around.

"You be careful out there," Emala urged. "What with buffalo and bears and snakes and things, this country is enough to give a body fits."

"Stay here until I get back. It should not take long." Winona goaded her mare.

The tracks were plain enough. Chickory had gone east, back the way they came, staying close to the river so he wouldn't lose his way. *Smart of the boy*, Winona mused. It made his absence more puzzling.

Winona rode with her Hawken cradled in the crook of her elbow. She wasn't overly worried. There hadn't been any sign of hostiles. Nor had she heard any shots or roars or screams. Whatever had happened to the boy, she was sure it would turn out to be something minor. Maybe he had just lost track of time. Maybe he had climbed down from his horse for some reason, and the horse had wandered off. It could be any number of things.

Winona smiled as she rode. She was fond of the Platte. It wasn't much as rivers went; in the mountains it would be called a stream. But it flowed year round, and in the driest months it was the only source of water to be had over hundreds of miles of prairie. All sorts of animals depended on that water.

The oaks, cottonwoods and willows were home to squirrels and birds. The brush was home to deer and elk. Rabbits were everywhere. Raccoons, skunks and opossums roamed its banks at night. Herds of buffalo came to drink, churning the water brown and trampling the vegetation.

Winona spied a pair of ducks paddling quaintly in a pool. A male and female, judging by their markings. Mallards, her husband called them. They betrayed no alarm. She wanted to stop and admire them, but she had the boy to find.

The tracks continued to point east.

Winona figured it was safe to cup a hand to her mouth. "Chickory? Chickory Worth? Where are you?

Other than the twittering of sparrows, there was no answer.

Winona leaned down. She had found where the boy rode fast, and soon she came on the cause. Chickory was after a buck. She knew it was a buck because she found where it had urinated. Does always squatted. This deer hadn't.

Winona admired his gumption if not his judgment. Bucks were extremely wary. To get close enough for a shot took considerable skill, skill the boy didn't have. Odds were the buck would tire of the cat-and-mouse game and vanish, if it hadn't already.

A jay squawked and was mimicked by another. Winona saw them fly from tree to tree. Raiding nests to eat the hatchlings, she reckoned, as did crows and ravens, which was why the three were at the bottom of her list of favorite birds.

Winona rounded a bend—and drew rein in surprise. Directly ahead, its reins tied to a bush, was Chickory's horse—but no Chickory. She called his name but got no reply.

Winona kneed her mare up next to the sorrel and slid down. She shouted the boy's name again. Puzzled, she walked in a circle around the sorrel. The sorrel's tracks went past where it was tied and then came back again. Evidently, Chickory had ridden past this point, returned, tied his horse to the bush, and gone on afoot.

Why would he do that? Winona wondered. The only answer she could think of was that he was stalking the buck.

Winona started after him. She assumed he hadn't gone far, but she covered the distance three arrows could fly without spotting him. She stopped, debating whether to go on or wait there.

A low sound carried to her ears.

Winona couldn't quite identify it, but it might have been the groan of an animal in pain. Leveling her Hawken, she crept toward a cluster of cottonwoods. She scoured the ground for tracks and discovered the prints of other horses, all of them shod. She was bending to examine them when the groan was repeated.

Winona looked up, and her blood changed to ice water.

His arms outspread, Chickory Worth had been tied by his wrists to two cottonwoods. Someone had beaten him; blood trickled down his brow and red drops dribbled from his chin. He was barely conscious. He groaned a third time, and his eyelids fluttered.

Winona moved to help him.

That was when the undergrowth rustled and parted, and figures closed in from all sides.

Chapter Nine

It was a gorgeous, sunny day, painting the prairie in vivid hues with added splashes of color from wildflowers.

Nate King loved days like this—the sun warm on his face, the fragrances in the air. He breathed deep and felt some of the tension drain from him like water from a sieve.

Nate had spent the past two hours scouting the river for sign. He hadn't found any, hostile or otherwise. Drawing rein, he swung down. "We'll water the horses and then head back."

"Fine by me, hoss," Peleg Harrod said. He dismounted stiffly and put a hand to the small of his back. "These old bones of mine ain't what they used to be. Too much saddle and I'm a bundle of aches."

"You're spry enough for someone your age." Nate brought his bay to the water's edge. "My wife will be happy to hear there aren't any Sioux about. We've tangled with them a time or two."

"Who hasn't?" Harrod laughed. "They love to count coup on whites more than they love to count coup on just about anyone. Except maybe the Shoshones."

Nate grunted. The long-standing animosity between his adopted people and the Sioux was well known. "It's too bad all the tribes can't live in peace."

"Peace ain't human nature. Red or white, they live to make war." Harrod led his own horse over.

"Most folks I know favor peace over spilling blood."

"Maybe they say they do. But name me one time in all history when there wasn't a war somewhere. Killing is in our blood. Has been since Cain and Abel."

"So we forget about the part where it says 'Thou shalt not kill'?"

Harrod chortled. "This from a coon who, from what I hear, has sent a heap of souls into the here-after. Don't take this wrong, but you're a fine one to talk."

Nate squatted and dipped his hand in the river. He couldn't deny his past. But he could, and did, defend his deeds. "I've only ever taken a life when I had to."

"Is that a fact? Then that 'Thou shalt not kill' doesn't count when it's not convenient?"

"I don't know as I like your tone."

"Sorry. It's just that a lot of those who say they live as God wants them to live tend to break His rules as much as the rest of us."

Nate splashed water on his neck and felt cool drops trickle under his buckskin shirt and down his chest. "I can't argue with that. I'm only saying most people would be glad to go through their entire lives without taking someone else's."

Harrod picked up a small flat stone. He threw it, skipping it across the surface as boys were wont to do. "I'd have been content to go through my life that way. But it wasn't meant to be."

"Life never goes as we think it should."

"Ain't that the truth." Harrod picked up another flat stone and skipped it—four times before it sank. Searching for more, he came around the bay. "You probably never figured on nursemaidin' a black family, did you?"

Nate glanced up. "Why mention them?"

"No reason, except that it shows things happen to us we never plan on." Harrod bent and picked up a stone, but it wasn't flat enough and he dropped it. "Take me, for instance. I've done things I can't believe I did. Nearly always, I did them for money."

Nate set down his Hawken and dipped both hands in the water. "I try to get by with needing as little as I can."

"Wish I could. But I've got me a few vices. I like to drink. I like whiskey an awful lot. I like cards on occasion, and now and then I pay the painted ladies a visit. All that takes money."

"You could always give them up."

"I wish it were that simple. My vices are as much a part of me as whatever virtues I have." Harrod sighed. "Precious few, I'm afraid. No, I'll do just about anything for money except hurt women. That's the one thing I've never done and won't ever do."

Nate cupped water and pressed his hands to his face and welcomed the relief it brought from the heat. Through his fingers he said, "But you'd hurt a man for money. Is that what you're telling me?"

Harrod selected a rock as big as his fist. "As a matter of fact, it is. I'm being paid extra in this case, seeing as how the man is more dangerous than most and the gents who hired me want him alive."

"'This case'?" Nate started to turn. He saw the frontiersman's reflection in the water, saw Harrod's arm sweep down, and the back of his head exploded with pain.

His last sensation was of pitching into black emptiness.

"Well, this a fine *how do you do*," Emala complained. "Our Chickory went missing. Mrs. King went after him and never came back. And now Mr. King and that Harrod are overdue." In her anxiety she plucked at her dress and fiddled with a button.

"Want me to go look for them, Ma?" Randa volunteered.

"And have you taken captive by some red devil? I should say not." Emala planted her thick legs. "The three of us will stay right where we are until someone shows up."

Samuel had been quiet a while, but now he said, "I don't think that's smart."

"What would you suggest?"

Samuel stared to the west at the reddish orange ball a few hours from setting. "It's been so long, they must be in some kind of trouble. You two wait here while I go look for Chickory and Mrs. King."

"Without a gun? What will you do if they *are* in danger? If it's Indians, you wouldn't stand a prayer."

"We can't sit here doin' nothin'." Samuel turned to the horses, but he only took a step when his wife had his arm in a vise.

"No, you don't. I've lost my boy today and I'm not losin' my husband, too. The only way you're gettin' on that animal is if you lift me up with you."

"I'm strong but I'm not that strong."

Randa, anxious to end their bickering, stepped between them. "Why don't we go together?"

That was what they did, in single file, with Samuel in the lead and Randa bringing up the rear.

Emala gazed about them with eyes as wide as saucers. "Lordy. I see now why you like havin' that gun. These woods are spooky even in the daylight. We never know but that one of them big bears or a bunch of hungry wolves or a pack of them big cats will jump us."

Randa said, "Mrs. King told me they're called mountain lions. And they don't go around in packs."

"How can they be *mountain* lions when the highest thing we've seen in weeks was a puny hill? Maybe they're mountain lions in the mountains, but here they're prairie lions or maybe plains lions or even grass lions, but they sure ain't mountain lions."

"I could use wax to plug my ears," Samuel said.

Emala took exception. "There you go again, speakin' ill of me. And you don't even have the courtesy to do it behind my back."

Randa wished she had some wax, too. She remembered how nice her parents were to each other back when they were slaves, and she wondered why they argued so much now that they were free. It seemed to her it should be the other way around. She shut out their squabbling and admired the scenery. The blue-green of the river, the various greens of the trees, yet another shade of green for the grass, and over all the brilliant blue of the sky. She never saw anything like this back on the plantation.

Nate King had told her that the sky back east was different from the sky in the west. How that could be, Randa couldn't fathom. To her, sky was sky. Why should it change from one place to another?

Out in the river a fish broke the surface, spawning

ripples. Randa couldn't begin to guess what kind it was. In Georgia she had known every animal and plant by name. Out here so much was new, it was like learning how to live all over again.

A big yellow and black butterfly fluttered past, and Randa grinned. To find such beauty in the midst of so many perils . . . Winona King mentioned once that there were just as many dangers in the mountains, but that the valley they were bound for was a paradise where they could live in peace the rest of their days.

Randa would believe it when she saw it. From the time when she was old enough to remember, life had been hard. Granted, the most danger she was ever in as a slave was when Master Brent took a liking to her. But no place on earth could be as wonderful as Winona King made King Valley out to be.

Suddenly Randa realized her mother was talking to her.

". . . bad enough your father treats me so shabby, I won't have it from my children. Now you answer me and you answer me this second. You don't want me riled."

"Sorry, Ma," Randa said. "I was thinkin' of how our life was before we ran away."

"No sense in livin' in the past, girl. We're free now and we'll have to make the best of it."

Samuel said quietly, "Hush, woman."

"There you go *again*!" Emala was stupefied. "Now that we're free I will talk when I feel like talkin' and there isn't a thing—"

By then Samuel had turned his horse, reached out, and clamped a hand over her mouth. "Hush!" he said again. "Someone is comin'."

They all heard the thud of hooves. Riders were approaching at a gallop. Quickly, Samuel reined toward the Platte River. Up ahead, part of the bank had washed away, leaving a drop of some ten feet. He rode to the cutoff and motioned for his wife and daughter to do as he was doing.

Emala balked. "Will you look at him? Hidin' down there when it could be Mrs. King and our Chickory."

"It could be Indians, too," Randa said.

Emala ficked her reins and flapped her legs and got her horse down next to Samuel's.

Samuel placed a hand on his belt where his pistol should be. He moved it to the hilt of his knife.

The drumming grew louder.

Samuel bent low. Randa copied him, but Emala sat there straight as she could sit. "Get down, woman."

"I have a cramp."

"What?"

"In my leg. From when I slapped it against this horse. It hurts somethin' awful."

Randa asked, "Would you rather it was an arrow in your leg, Ma?"

Emala bent, but she wasn't happy about it. She wasn't built for bending. She was too thick across the middle—she liked to think of herself as pleasantly plump—and besides, her bosoms were so big that she had to press them against the horse's neck and get its sweat all over them. The only sweat she liked was her own. "What did I ever do to deserve all this sufferin'?"

Then the bank seemed to shake and the water to stir and riders flew past above them.

Samuel twisted his head to look. He counted four, all white, men he never saw before. One was short and one was young and another had a bushy mustache and held a shotgun. The last man had a hard cast to his face. They went by fast, staring straight ahead.

Samuel waited until the thunder died, then straightened. "I didn't like the looks of that bunch."

"Me neither," Emala said. "Praise the Lord they didn't see us. We have enough troubles."

"What worries me," Randa said, "is that they were comin' from the direction Chickory and Mrs. King went."

"We best keep goin'." Samuel rode along the bank to a grassy incline, and up it into the trees. He twisted in the saddle. The four men were nowhere to be seen. "We were lucky."

"Luck had nothin' to do with it," Emala disagreed. "I keep tellin' you the Lord is lookin' after us. I prayed, and He made us invisible."

"That is the silliest notion you've ever come up with, and you have come up with some whoppers."

"I'll whopper you, oh ye of little faith. The Lord is our rock and our salvation." When Samuel didn't say anything, Emala prompted him with, "Well?"

"No, you don't. Every time you bring religion into things, I get a blisterin' that would bring Samson to his knees."

"At least you remember his name. Given how little you read Scripture, that's somethin'."

"See what I mean?" Samuel said to Randa.

" 'Unto thee will I cry, oh Lord, my rock,' " Emala quoted. " 'Be not silent to me, lest, if thou be silent to me, I become like them that go down into the pit. Here the voice of my supplications when I cry unto thee, when I lift up my hands toward thy holy oracle. Draw me not away with the wicked, and with the workers of iniquity.' "

"I'd sure like to know the Bible as good as you do, Ma," Randa said, with a wink at her father.

"It's taken a lifetime of study, child. If more people kept their nose in the Word and out of the affairs of others, this world would be a lot nicer place."

Fresh clods of dirt marked the trail. Samuel studied the tracks, trying to make sense of them. Nate King had promised to teach him how to read sign. He couldn't wait. He was so intent on the ground that he didn't realize the trail was blocked until his horse stopped and nickered.

Samuel looked up.

"Dear God!" Emala blurted.

Not ten feet away, lying on their backs and bound hand and foot and gagged, was their son and Winona King.

Chapter Ten

"Chickory!" Randa cried, and started to goad her horse up past her mother's to reach her brother.

Emala was struck speechless; the unexpected always unnerved her, and this was as unexpected as could be.

Samuel started to swing down. Suddenly he was aware of men on foot closing in from all sides. "Look out!" he shouted to his wife and his daughter.

Randa hauled on her reins. She didn't want to leave, but instinct warned her that if she didn't escape, she would end up trussed and helpless. A short man snatched at her bridle, but she jabbed her heels and her horse knocked him aside.

"Stop her!"

Samuel was torn between helping his son and Mrs. King, and fleeing. He started to dismount, thought better of it, and swung his leg back again. But before he could use his reins, two of the men reached him. The one on the right had a bristly mustache and was holding a shotgun, but made no attempt to use it. The one on the left had blond hair and cold blue eyes. Each grabbed one of Samuel's legs.

Emala squealed in panic. Two men were converging on her. "No, you don't!" she cried, and reined around. She smacked her horse with the flat of her hand and it broke into a gallop. Pleased with herself, she suddenly realized she was riding toward a low limb. She ducked, but she couldn't duck low enough; her bosoms got in the way. She tried to twist aside, but the limb caught her across the shoulder. The next thing she knew, she was on her back on the ground with the breath whooshed from her lungs and a short man and a young man standing over her and grinning.

"You sure made that easy, you tub of lard."

Still on his horse, Samuel kicked the man with the mustache and jerked his leg free of the blond man. He sought to flee. He would have made it, too, except he saw his wife fall and he reined over to help her. That was when another white man, a burly brute with a beard, came hurtling out of the undergrowth. Samuel recognized him; it was a slave hunter called Trumbo. Trumbo rammed into him like a two-legged battering ram.

To his dismay, Samuel was unhorsed.

Fifty feet into the trees, Randa looked back and saw that her father and mother were down. She almost turned back to help them, but the youngest of the whites whipped out a pistol and took aim at her. There was no doubt he would have shot her except that another man appeared, a man she had encountered before—Wesley, his name was—and swatted the younger man's arm. The pistol went off, but the ball dug a furrow in the ground and not through her.

Randa kept riding.

Emala was on her back, but she wasn't helpless. She kicked the short man trying to seize her.

Cursing fiercely, the man backed off and leveled

his rifle. "Try that again and I will by-God shoot you!"

"Lower that weapon," Wesley commanded. "How many times must I tell you that they are worth more to me alive than they are dead?"

Samuel barely heard that. He was too busy fighting. Trumbo had slammed him onto his back and sought to pin him, but Samuel was just as big and a lot stronger. He gave the bearded man-bear a shove that sent Trumbo flying. Before Samuel could rise, the man with the mustache and the man with the yellow hair were on him. They got hold of his arms, and the blond man tried to bend his arm behind his back.

Bellowing like a mad bull, Samuel threw them off and heaved to his feet. He turned to help Emala.

"Not another step," Wesley said, jamming the muzzle of his Kentucky against Samuel's thigh. "Shooting you in the leg won't kill you, but it will sure as hell tame you."

Samuel froze.

"The girl got away," Trumbo said.

"She won't get far," Wesley predicted. "As soon as we tie these two, I want you and Bromley and Kleist to go after her. She's heading for the open prairie, so it shouldn't be hard to catch her."

Emala sat up and jabbed a finger at the backwoodsman. "I should have known it would be you!"

"You're money in my poke, woman," Wesley replied. "A lot of money. I wasn't about to give up this side of the hereafter." He backed away from Samuel but held the Kentucky on him. "Listen good, you Worths. So long as you do what I say, when I say, you'll make it back to Georgia in one piece. Give me trouble, any at all, and you'll suffer."

Samuel was quivering with fury. He thought the slave hunters had given up, but here they were again. But there was no way he was going back again. No way in hell. He would rather be dead than a slave. Besides, they weren't taking him back to put him to work in the cotton fields. They were taking him back to hang him.

Trumbo went into the trees and reappeared leading horses. From one he took a coiled rope and came over. "Turn around and put your hands behind you."

Samuel did no such thing.

"You heard him," Wesley said. "Or is it that you want me to shoot your wife?" He trained the Kentucky on Emala.

"No. Don't hurt her. I'll do what you want."

"Oh, Samuel," Emala said.

It was just about the hardest thing Samuel ever had to do. He hated it, hated having rope looped tight around his wrists, hated being made to sit and have his ankles tied, too.

"Now do his wife," Wesley directed.

Emala balled a pudgy fist. "Just you try it," she warned. "I'll bean you on the nose. You just see if I don't."

Wesley sighed. "Do you have a lick of sense?"

"I don't care if you put lead into me. I ain't bein' tied and that's all there is to it."

"Then how about if I put lead into your man?" Wesley aimed at Samuel's leg.

"All right. All right." Emala held out her wrists. "Why are all slave hunters so vile?"

"I'm just doing my job, woman. How easy or hard it is depends on you. Keep that in mind and we'll get along fine."

Emala fought down a wave of fear. She turned to Winona King and said softly, "I'm sorry to get you mixed up in this. I truly am."

Winona tried to spit out the gag but couldn't.

Chuckling, Olan walked over and yanked it out for her. "Usually I don't give a lick about squaws. But you're so pretty I'll make an exception."

"Pig." Winona shifted toward Wesley. "My husband will come after us. And he will not be alone. If you are smart, you will let us go and ride away while you still can."

"I'm smarter than you think," Wesley told her.

At that, all of their captors laughed.

Pain. A lot of pain. It told Nate King he had returned to the land of the living, although given the throbbing in his head, it might have been better if he stayed unconscious. He felt a swaying motion and something gouging his gut. He must be belly-down over a saddle. He tried to move his arms and legs, and couldn't.

"I tie good knots," Peleg Harrod said. "You can open your eyes. I know you've come around."

Nate blinked in the bright sun and turned his head. The old frontiersman was leading his bay by the reins. "Why?"

"That's the first question I would ask, too. The answer is simple. Money."

"Someone paid you to bash me over the head?"

"They paid me to lead you into a trap so they can shoot you. The head bash was my idea. You'll find this hard to believe, but I've done you a favor."

"You're right. It is hard to believe." The pain was making a jumble of Nate's thoughts.

"You'll savvy when I tell you who I work for."

Harrod paused. "Does the handle Wesley mean any-thing to you?"

In a rush of memory Nate relived his clash weeks ago with the slave hunters after the Worths. "I fig-ured we were safe once we crossed the Mississippi River."

"You figured wrong. Those blacks are worth a lot of money. I'm not talking hundreds. I'm talking thousands."

"You weren't with them when we tangled back in Missouri."

"Wesley hired me later. Me and some others who are a lot worse than me. We don't get along much on account of I have scruples and they don't."

Nate tested the rope around his wrists. It didn't have any slack. The same with the rope around his ankles. To keep the older man talking, he said in mock surprise, "You have scruples?"

"That was uncalled for. But I won't harm females. Ever. And I won't kill unless I have to. I failed to mention that to Wesley. He took it for granted I'd have no qualms about leading you into an ambush."

"So you're a cutthroat, but a nice cutthroat?"

"Hell, I'm no cutthroat at all. I used to be a trap-per, like you. Now I mostly guide and scout and track and such. This Wesley hired me to tag along with him because he's never been west of the Mis-sissippi."

Nate's head was beginning to clear, although it still throbbed. "Do you suppose I could impose on these scruples of yours and you could cut me loose?"

"I would like to. I honest to God would. I've grown fond of you and that wife of yours. You're fine folks. As fine as I've ever met."

"But . . . ?" Nate prompted when Harrod didn't go on.

"But if I let you go you'll go charging off to help the blacks and get yourself killed. I'm doing you another favor by keeping you tied."

"You're full of favors I can do without."

Peleg Harrod chortled. "Now see, most men would be foaming at the mouth about now. They'd be cussing and kicking and saying as how they'd like nothing better than to slit my throat. But not you. You lie there as calm as can be. You even joke about what I did to you."

"So far all you did was conk me on the noggin. Set me free and there won't be any hard feelings."

"I didn't fall off the turnip wagon yesterday. You're only saying that because you want to go after your wife and the blacks."

"Those blacks have a name."

Harrod shifted to stare quizzically at him. "Don't get me wrong, I'm not like Wesley and his bunch. I don't hate blacks just because they're not white. Hell, I've had me a few Injun wives."

"But . . . ?" Nate said again.

"But I don't give a good damn what happens to them. They never did trust me."

"After what they've been through, can you blame them?"

Harrod grinned and wagged a finger. "Don't try to make me feel sorry for them. Sure, they're decent folks. And yes, they must have had it rough as slaves. But Samuel killed a man. He up and murdered his master. He deserves whatever they dish out."

"Have you ever killed?"

Harrod nodded. "I've had to blow out a few wicks. A couple of times so I could keep my hair on my head. And once or twice because someone thought they could help themselves to my horse or my poke."

"Did you know that Samuel Worth killed his owner to keep his daughter from being raped."

"Damn you to hell."

"What?"

"It won't work."

"What won't?"

Abruptly drawing rein, Harrod reined his horse around and brought it next to the bay. "You are one devious son of a bitch, do you know that? Trying to convince me to side with the Worths."

"I only told you what happened." But the truth was, Nate did hope to change the frontiersman's mind.

"And money grows on trees and the moon is made of cheese." Harrod made a clucking sound. "I don't want another word out of you—not so much as a peep. Do you hear me?"

"What if I promise not to talk about the Worths?"

"Not about the Worths, or about slaves, or about slave hunters, or about slavery, or about how life ain't fair, or about my scruples."

"Is that all?"

"No. You're not to talk about your wife or your kids if you have any or bring up Jesus or God or your parson if you have one or talk about how the human heart is tender or fickle or both."

"Is there anything left?

Harrod blinked, then laughed and slapped his leg. "Don't you beat all. But I mean it. No tricky talk." He gigged his mount and resumed heading east.

Nate flexed his arms. The rope dug into his wrists, but he didn't care. He had to work loose no matter how much it hurt or how long it took. "You mentioned having wives—"

"You can' talk about them, either."

"Did you have any children?"

"Nor them."

"How about pets? You must have had a dog or cat you were fond of. Or maybe you're partial to that horse you're riding."

Harrod swung around. "When I said you were devious, I didn't know the half of it. All right. From here on out you're not to speak unless I speak to you first."

"That's awful harsh."

"It will be harsher if I have to gag you."

"Can I say one last thing?"

Harrod groaned.

"My wife thought highly of you." Nate seldom lied. In fact, he could count the number of times he had lied on one hand and have fingers left over. But he was lying now. "How can you let them hurt her?"

Peleg Harrod swore. "I should have led you into that ambush like they wanted."

Chapter Eleven

In her panic Randa didn't realize which direction she had fled until she burst from the vegetation that bordered the Platte River and beheld an unending vista of prairie. She didn't stop. For all she knew they were after her. She had to get away so she could come back later and do what she could to help her family and Winona. That was her overriding thought as she slapped her legs against her mount, goading it to a gallop.

Randa glanced back. She was puzzled that none of the slave hunters was after her. For a few happy seconds she thought she had escaped. Then she glanced back again—and three riders emerged from the trees. One was the burly bear with a beard, Trumbo. The others were the blond man and the man with the shotgun. Trumbo rose in the stirrups, spotted her and pointed. All three immediately gave chase.

Randa hoped her parents and brother were all right. The fact that they were worth more alive than dead suggested they would be. But she had heard awful stories about the terrible things slaves hunters had done to runaways, and her heart was heavy with worry.

When Randa next looked over her shoulder, the three men hadn't gained on her. A grim grin curled her lips. They were in for a surprise, those three, if they thought she would be easy to catch.

Randa galloped for another half mile. Then several things occurred to her. First, she was on the open prairie. There was nowhere to hide even if she should widen her lead. Second, her horse—a skewbald, Nate King called it—was breathing heavier than she had ever heard it breathe. And third, the men after her were holding to the same steady pace, so she didn't dare slow down. Put those three together and it told her they were deliberately trying to—what was the expression?—ride her horse into the ground.

Randa would be the first to admit she didn't know a lot about horses. For instance, how far could they go without tiring? At a walk, probably all day. But at a gallop? She figured five or ten miles, but she could be mistaken. She slowed anyway and glanced back again.

The three were still after her at that same steady gait.

Randa faced front and stiffened. Something strange was up ahead. Dark bumps lined the horizon. The bumps grew until she could see they were animals—big animals. There were a lot of them, too. She thought they might be elk until she remembered Nate King telling her that elk herds seldom numbered more than fifty or sixty. There looked to be hundreds of whatever was up ahead, scattered in clusters and singly.

Randa considered going around, but that would take precious time and cost her much of her lead on her pursuers.

Some of the animals heard her horse and raised their great shaggy heads.

A tingle of apprehension rippled down Randa's spine. She wanted to smack herself for not realizing what they were sooner. How could she not when she had nearly been gored by one? Their huge heads, their curved horns, their funny tails with the tufts at the end; they were buffalo.

Lots and lots of buffalo.

Randa's mouth went dry. The buff she had run into at the river had shown her how fierce they could be. And that had been just one. What was she to do against hundreds?

Randa went to rein wide of a bull that was stamping its front feet.

Then she saw that the three slave hunters had halved the distance. She had no choice but to go through the herd.

A bull grunted and pawed the ground.

A cow with a calf took a few steps in her direction and stamped and shook her head as if about to attack.

"What do I do? What do I do?" Randa asked the empty air.

The skewbald stopped.

Randa jabbed with her heels to get it moving. Suddenly a bull came toward them, its head lowered.

Randa tensed for a charge. She would try to outride it, even though Nate King had told her that buffalo were as fast as horses over short spurts.

The bull abruptly snorted and wheeled and trotted off.

Randa used her heels. The skewbald slowly

moved forward, but it was trembling with fear. She tried to get it to go faster, but it balked. She didn't blame it. Buffalo were on all sides now, some staring, some grazing. They were spaced far enough apart that if she was careful she might make it through without being attacked.

A calf came prancing toward her.

Randa drew rein and was on the watch for its mother. She motioned. "Shoo! Go away!"

The calf paid no heed. It tossed its head and bobbed its tail, reminding Randa of herself when she was seven or eight and she would go skipping down the lane.

The calf came within half a dozen feet, sniffed several times, and let out a bleat.

Almost instantly there came an answering bellow. From out of a group of cows came one in particular, raising puffs of dust with her heavy hooves.

Randa went to rein out of there when she remembered another kernel of frontier lore Nate King once shared: animals are drawn to movement. When confronted by a bear or a mountain lion, the worst thing a person can do is run. Randa imagined the same applied to a mother buffalo.

The calf pranced in a circle around the skewbald, perhaps drawn to it out of curiosity. It didn't seem to hear its mother's bellows, and if it did, it had a lot in common with human children—it ignored her.

"Go away, darn you!"

At the sound of her voice the calf uttered another sharp bleat and scampered away. The mother went after it, veering wide of the skewbald.

Randa let out the breath she had not realized she was holding. But her relief was short lived.

Another buffalo was coming to investigate. This time it was a huge bull in its prime. Head lowered, it rumbled and snorted and gouged the ground.

Randa figured that if she sat there quietly the bull would leave her be. She didn't count on the skewbald doing the last thing it should; whinnying in fear and bolting.

"No!" Randa cried, and hauled on the reins. But the skewbald refused to stop. Worse, it was galloping toward a group of twenty or more buffs, bunched so close together that a goat couldn't get through, let alone a horse.

"Whoa!" Randa shouted. She heard drumming hooves and looked behind her. Her heart leaped into her throat.

The big bull had given chase and was hard on the skewbald's flank. Should the horse slow, even a little bit, the bull would be on them in the blink of an eye.

Hugging the horse's back, Randa gave it a smack. She hollered, thinking it might scatter the buffalo they were heading toward. A few looked up, but the rest, amazingly, paid no more attention than if she were a prairie dog. "Get out of the way!" she screamed.

A few did. The rest stood chewing and staring or, as one buffalo was doing, rolling around in the dirt.

Randa was certain she was done for. The bull would catch her or the ones in front would turn on her. Either way, she was dead. In desperation she did the only thing she could think of: she hauled on the reins with all her might.

The bull thundered past, its horn missing the skewbald by a whisker. It plowed into the others, snorting and swinging its head, and they scattered in all directions, their tails held high.

Several passed so close to Randa that she could have reached out and touched them. The skewbald stood still, but quaked.

Then the buffalo were gone, and dust settled around her. She let out another sign of relief. Once again it was short lived.

"Damn, girl. Are you *trying* to get yourself killed?" Randa wrenched her head around.

The three slave hunters had caught up. They sat their horses calmly, smirking.

"No!" Randa exclaimed.

"Oh, yes," said the man with the shotgun. He pointed it at her.

Winona King was mad. Not at those who had jumped her and bound her. She was mad at herself for being taken unawares. In the wilderness a person must always stay alert. Now here she was, tied hand and foot. Helpless, and in the clutches of men whose violent natures were mirrored in their cold, uncaring eyes.

Winona had been studying them and listening while they waited for the three called Trumbo, Bromley and Kleist to return. She remembered Wesley from before. Olan and Cranston were new to her. The former was a strutting fool, always belligerent, always angry. The latter was a boy in a man's clothes, but a vicious boy who had never learned that kindness was a worthwhile trait.

Winona shifted to relieve a kink in her leg and caught Wesley studying her even as she had studied them. "Yes?"

"You sure are a thinker, squaw. I'll give that to you."

"How about if we make a deal?" Winona requested. "You will not call me squaw and I will not call you son of a bitch." She recalled that white men did not like that; they did not like that at all.

Olan howled with delight. "Ain't she something? She talks better than I do and she's a redskin, for God's sake."

"I can kick her teeth in if you want," Cranston said eagerly.

Wesley, cradling his Kentucky, shot the younger man a glare of annoyance. "I'm tired of telling you to leave them be."

"I thought it was the blacks you don't want touched? You didn't say anything about no Injuns."

"She stays alive and unharmed," Wesley said. "At least until we bag her husband. He won't lay a finger on us so long as we have her."

"Scared of him, are you?" Cranston snickered.

In a blur Wesley was on him. He shoved the Kentucky's stock in the younger man's gut and Cranston doubled over, gasping. He thrust out a hand to ward off another blow to the ribs, and Wesley clubbed him in the head instead.

Cranston sprawled, unconscious.

"Was that necessary?" Olan asked.

Wesley spun. "You heard him. I'm tired of playing nursemaid. He's one of yours. That's your job. Have a talk with him or the next time he gets a slug between the eyes."

"That's the first threat I ever heard you make."

"It wasn't a threat," Wesley corrected. He turned back to Winona. "Now, where were we? That's right. I was saying how you impress me. You're smart for a female, red or white."

"I was smart enough to marry a good man who will not rest until you are six feet under."

"I might have a surprise for you. Has this good

man of yours ever taught you a game called checkers?"

"Checkers and chess and other games besides. We have spent many an evening playing them."

"Then you know that the key to winning at checkers is to remove the other player's pieces. And that's exactly what I've done with your husband."

Fear filled Winona, but she did not let it show. Another thing she had learned from the man she loved was something called a poker face. "Removed him how?"

"You'll find out soon enough." Wesley turned to the Worths. "How about you three? Cat got your tongues? You can talk if you want, so long as you talk civil."

"I hate you," Emala said. "And I'll hate you more if anything happens to my baby girl. You hear me?"

"Spare me, lady."

"I am, you know."

"Am what?"

"A lady. I trust you and your friends will remember that and not try to take liberties."

Olan, who was helping Cranston up, let out a snort. "Poke a darkie? That'll be the day."

"You're perfectly safe in that regard," Wesley assured her.

"Poking you would be like poking a hog or a cow," Olan added.

Chickory started to come up off the ground but found himself looking at the Kentucky's muzzle. "Don't talk to my ma like that! She *is* a lady, you hear?" He twisted toward his father, who sat with his arms over his knees and his head bowed. "Pa? Didn't you hear him? Say somethin', will you?"

Samuel didn't respond.

"What's the matter? They didn't hurt you, did they?"

"I thought we were free, son. Finally and truly free. I thought we would have a place of our own and be happy."

"What does that have to do with how he insulted Ma? He called her a hog and a cow."

"I've never been so happy as these past weeks. I could do what I wanted. I could hold my head high and say I'm a man."

"Of course you're a man. What else would you be?"

Winona was concerned for Samuel. All the fight and much of the life seemed to have drained from his hardy frame. He hadn't said a word until now. It wasn't his body that was broken so much as his spirit. "We must never give up, never lose hope," Winona said.

"Even if my family and me got away from this bunch, they'd only send more after us. There's no escape."

"I've been telling you that all along," Wesley said.

"It's all that wool between his ears," Olan taunted.

Just then hooves thudded to the west, and around a bend in the trail came riders.

Olan grinned and pointed. "No one escapes us for long."

Chapter Twelve

For hours Nate King had worked at loosening the ropes that bound his wrists and ankles, but he didn't have much luck. The rope around his wrists yielded enough for him to wiggle his forearms, but the rope around his ankles was knotted too tight.

It would have to do. Nate couldn't wait much longer. They could come on the slave hunters at any time. Again and again he raised his head as high as he could and scoured the terrain ahead for a place to make his move. So far, providence wasn't being kind.

Presently Harrod slowed and rode with extra caution.

Nate could guess why. They were near the clearing where he had left Winona and the Worths.

"Well, that's peculiar," Harrod remarked.

"What is?"

"Take a gander."

Ahead was the clearing. It was empty.

"Where could they have gotten to?" Nate wondered aloud.

"How should I know?" Harrod appeared genuinely puzzled. "I haven't left your side all day." He let go of the bay's reins and rode in a circle, examining the ground. "Looks to me as if they just up and rode off, back the way we came."

"Why would they do that?" Nate knew Winona as well as he knew himself. She must have had a compelling reason. But for the life of him, he couldn't think of what.

Harrod contemplated the woods. "My first thought was that the Sioux drove them off, but we'd have heard something."

Nate decided the time had come. "Maybe it was. The Sioux are clever about hiding their tracks." He looked up and pretended to give a start. Pointing with both hands across the river, he yelled, "Look! There's a bunch of Sioux over yonder!"

Harrod fell for the ruse. He snapped around in the saddle, blurting, "Where?"

Nate smacked his arms against one side of the bay and his legs against the other and the bay did what most every horse would do—it broke into a gallop, flying out of the clearing and along the trail to the east.

Harrod bellowed for him to stop.

"Fat chance!" Nate yelled back. The jostling was ferocious. The saddle horn gouged his ribs. He bit at the knots on the rope around his wrist, but he had no more success than before.

"Consarn you, King! How far do you think you'll get?" Harrod shouted after him.

A good long way, if Nate had any say. He would have a minute, maybe two, before Harrod caught up. They swept around a bend; on the left was a grassy incline lapped by a pool.

Giving the bay another whack, Nate pushed off from the saddle. He landed on his shoulder, the grass cushioning him, and rolled. Wetness wrapped him in its embrace—he was on his belly in the Platte. He scrambled backward. The water rose to his nose, to his eyes. Hooves drummed up above. Taking a deep breath, he hugged the bottom.

A murky caricature of a horse and rider sped past the bank.

Nate heaved onto his knees. Dripping wet, he hopped out. It wouldn't take Harrod long to discover his trick. The instant the old frontiersman saw the bay without him, Harrod would rein around and hunt for him.

Nate scrabbled up the incline. He slipped, surged higher, slipped again. Digging his toes in, he reached the top.

As yet there was no sign of Harrod.

Regaining his feet, Nate hopped across the trail into the woods. A tree loomed. He tried to avoid it but ran into the trunk. Pain flared. Then he was on all fours, plunging as deep into a thicket as he could go. Thorns raked his cheek, his neck. One nearly took out an eye.

Every muscle aquiver, Nate settled onto his side. He waited for his breathing to steady, then renewed his assault on the knots. They refused to give. He bit so hard, it felt as if his teeth would break.

To the east hooves pounded.

Nate flattened. He couldn't see the trail, but he glimpsed the old man's silhouette.

"King? Where are you? I've got your horse."

Nate gnawed at the rope.

"I know you can hear me. You have to be around here somewhere. Pretty clever, what you did. But now you're on foot. You don't have any weapons. Think of what that means."

Nate went on gnawing. It was common knowledge that a man afoot was an early grave waiting to happen.

"What's this?" Harrod exclaimed.

The silhouette had stopped near the grassy slope.

Nate dug his top teeth into a knot and pried. It gave a fraction but no more.

"So this is where you jumped off? You muddied the water. And here's a track."

It puzzled Nate, Harrod talking so much. Did the man really think he would answer? Or was there more to it? He stopped gnawing and peered through the thicket. All he saw was greenery and a patch of blue sky.

A twig crunched.

Moccasins appeared. Harrod was moving slowly, apparently wary of being jumped.

Nate didn't move a muscle.

The moccasins stopped, and Harrod called out, "Listen, King. You can't have gotten far. I suspect you can hear me. So here's something for you to think about." Harrod paused. "Your wife."

Nate's fingers clenched as they would if he had them around a throat and was throttling the life from someone.

"I told you about Wesley. He's no bluff. He wants those blacks and he will have them. And he won't let anyone stand in his way. Not you. Not your missus." Harrod waited for a reply, and when Nate didn't say anything, he said, "It could be Wesley has her. It could be he has all of them, and he's waiting for me to show up with you."

Nate glanced at the empty knife sheath on his hip.

"I know how one like him thinks. He'll keep your woman alive only so long as it suits his purpose.

Then he'll hand her over to the others. You haven't met them yet. They're animals. They'll gladly slit her throat after they've had their way."

An image of Winona enduring the unspeakable set Nate's blood to boiling. He grew warm all over.

"Wesley might give her to them anyway if I show up without you just to spite you. Or maybe he'll set her out as bait to lure you in." The moccasins turned in a circle. "Where the blazes are you? Why do I feel your eyes on me?"

To vent his anger, Nate resumed his assault on the knots.

"Come out of hiding and I promise there will be no hard feelings. I'll even cut your ankles free so you can sit your saddle. What do you say?"

Nate touched his belt where his flintlocks should be.

"I thought you cared for her," Harrod persisted.

Nate bit off an oath.

"The way you went on about how nice she is and all, I didn't think you'd want them to do the kinds of things they're going to do to her. What will it be? Don't you want to spare your woman a fate worse than death?"

The blazing orb men called the sun had followed its daily arc and was dipping toward the horizon. Streaks of pink, red and orange lent beauty to the sunset.

Winona was in no frame of mind to appreciate it. She was winding through the woods on foot, her wrists bound behind her back. A rope was around her neck and linked to Emala, who in turn was linked to Samuel. After him came Chickory and Randa.

"Dear Lord, save us," Emala prayed. "I will sing

of Your power. Yes, I will sing aloud of Your mercy in the morning." She sighed wearily. "That last was from the Bible, Mrs. King."

"My husband reads it nearly every night."

"So he told me. You have a good man there."

"Yes," Winona softly agreed. "A very good man."

"I read the Bible a lot myself. Not Samuel, though. He's not as religious as me. Fact is, there are days when I wonder if he has any religion at all."

Winona glanced past Emala at her husband, who walked with his head bowed. "How about that, Samuel? Do you believe in God, or what my people call the Great Mystery?"

"I used to."

Emala rolled her eyes. "If faith were a flame, I'd be a roarin' fire and he'd be a candle. If it were stone, I'd be a boulder and he'd be a pebble. Any faith this family has, I've had to nurture it like you would a seed."

"Oh, Lord, woman."

Emala clucked in reproach. "There you go again. Takin' the Lord in vain. Who knows the Bible inside and out? Me. Who can sing any song of praise you can think of? Me. Who prays mornin' and night that this family will be spared tribulation."

"Seems to me you need to pray harder."

"Samuel!"

A shadow fell over them. Wesley had reined his horse around. "Do you two bicker like this all the time?"

"Only lately," Emala said.

"I've listened to all I'm going to. Either talk nice or don't talk at all."

"If you don't mind my sayin'," Emala replied, "that sounds awful strange comin' from the likes of you. What you know about nice wouldn't fill a thimble."

For a moment Winona feared Wesley would strike her. Instead, he smiled.

"I get it now. You bicker with everyone."

"You don't know me," Emala said. "You only think you do. Sure, I've been out of sorts. But who can blame me with all that's happened?"

"This might surprise you, woman, but I don't blame you at all. It's not your fault your kind were dragged to this country. The slave traders are to blame. You should all be sent back to Africa, where you belong."

Emala shook her head. "I wouldn't know Africa from France. From what I hear, it's an awful place, with lions and tigers and snakes and people who eat other people. I was born in this country, just like my mother, and her mother before her, and I have no hankering to live anywhere else."

"You don't belong," Wesley said. "This country is for whites and only whites. Bringing your kind in was a mistake."

"The plantation owners don't think so. They work us like mules to put money in their pockets. Without us, they'd go broke."

"And there's the real reason you're here. It's always about the money."

As was their wont, songbirds and warblers filled the lush woodland with their paean to the departing day. Goldfinches with their clear notes, larks with perhaps the most musical calls of all, sparrows with their gay chirps, robins with their highs and lows, all combined in an avian chorus.

Normally, Winona enjoyed listening. But today she had something else on her mind.

Winona wasn't one to delude herself. She never looked at the bright side when there wasn't a bright side. The slave hunters had to kill her. Nate, too, if they caught him. They knew that she and Nate would do everything they could to stop them from taking the Worths back, even if that meant following them all the way back to the States.

Out of curiosity, Winona asked Wesley, "What are your plans for my husband and me?"

"That depends on you. Give me your word that if I let you go, you and your husband will head for the mountains and leave me free to collect the bounty on the darkies, and I'll cut you loose."

Winona hid her surprise. "You would trust me to do as you want?"

"I don't trust most people as far as I can heave them. But I've watched you close. For an Injun, a squaw, no less, you have more sand than most."

"I am flattered," Winona said. "And sad. The Worths are my friends. I cannot abandon them."

"Then you can't blame me for what's in store. I gave you your chance and you refused to take it." Wesley gigged his horse and rode to the front of the line with Trumbo and Olan. Cranston, Bromley and Kleist were at the rear.

Winona slowed and whispered to Emala, "We must try to get away the first chance we have."

"What are you talking about? We're tied and on foot. They have guns and are on horses. We can't get away unless you can help us all sprout wings."

"I didn't expect this of you."

"I have my family to think of. I don't want them harmed."

"We must try," Winona insisted.

Samuel raised his head and said so only they could hear, "Count me in. I'll do whatever it takes."

"Got your gumption back, did you?" Emala said. "Here I thought you gave up."

"Not this side of the grave. I'm over my sulk."

"What is it my husband read to me once? I remember. 'Give us liberty or give us death.'"

"Lord, help us," Emala said.

Winona smiled encouragement at Samuel. It was good to see him restored to his old self. Chickory and Randa would do what they had to, as well. But that begged the question: *what*? They were unarmed and bound. How were they to prevail over six killers bristling with weapons?

The answer came in the form of a whinny.

Chapter Thirteen

Nate King loved his wife more than anything. He loved her more than life. He loved her so deeply, she was part of him. He loved her so devotedly that when other women showed an interest, as had happened a few times, he politely but firmly made it as clear as clear could be that Winona was his one and only, now and forever.

Some men would call that silly. Some would call it stupid. Some would say that only a fool gave himself so completely to one woman. Some would deny there was even a thing like "love," and say that anyone who believed there was was fooling himself.

But Nate knew his heart and his mind, and when he was with Winona his heart was filled to overflowing with affection and his mind was filled with a deep sense of peace.

Love was real. Love was two hearts beating as one. Love was always caring, and always being there when the one you loved needed you.

Put more simply, Nate had found that Winona was his and he was hers, and that was how it was.

So to hear Harrod warn of what the slave hunters would do to her if he didn't give himself up tore at Nate as nothing else could. It hurt him where he could be hurt the most: in his heart. He was tempted, strongly tempted, to do as Harrod wanted. But a tiny urge at the back of his mind cautioned him not to.

If Harrod was right and the slave hunters had Winona, then it was up to Nate to stay free, and to free her. And then to deal with the slave hunters.

No one hurt those Nate cared for without paying in the same coin. No one harmed his family—or put any of them in harm's way—without being held accountable.

As Nate lay in the thicket listening to Peleg Harrod walk off, every fiber of his being burned with anger. Not so much at Harrod, although he'd liked the man and to a degree trusted him, despite Winona's misgivings. No, Nate was angry with himself for not heeding her. She'd warned him and he hadn't listened.

Nate renewed his attack on the knots. He pried and bit and tugged until his gums were bleeding and his whole mouth was sore. Bit by bit, slow degree by slow degree, he loosened the first of the knots. It took much too long. Daylight ebbed. The sun was on the rim of creation when the first knot came undone. Nate immediately went to work on the next. Either it wasn't as tight or he had learned from the first, but he got it undone in a tenth of the time.

Nate sat up and rubbed his wrists. There was still the rope around his ankles but it proved to be easy with his hands free.

He crawled out of the thicket and stood. A cool breeze fanned his face.

Night had fallen. The meat eaters were coming out of their dens and hidden places to prowl for prey. They filled the wild with their cries: coyotes yipped, a fox uttered a piercing shriek, to the west a grizzly snorted, and somewhere out on the prairie wolves howled.

Nate was no fool. He had lived in the wilderness long enough to know that a weapon meant the difference between living and dying. Any weapon would do. A lance. A bow. The only thing was, Harrod had taken his knife and his tomahawk, as well as his guns. Still, there were ways.

Nate made his way toward the Platte River. The myriad of stars lent a pale glow to the woodland. He could see to avoid trees and logs but not far enough ahead to tell whether an enemy, white or red, two-legged or four-legged, was slinking up on him

He came to the bank. Below, the river gurgled and burbled. He slid down, sank to his knees, and plunged in his hands. The water was wonderfully cool on his skinned wrists. It was also delicious. He drank his fill, then splashed some on his ankles.

Stones littered the bottom. Groping about, he found one he liked. It was the size of his fist, thick on one side and thin on the other. He chipped at the thin edge with another rock until it was sharp enough to suit him.

Next, Nate needed a downed limb. Preferably one about six feet long, fairly straight, that didn't require a lot of trimming. It took a while but he found one. He sharpened it as he hiked.

Harrod was long gone off to the east, back to those who had hired him. Nate bent his steps in the same direction. He figured—he hoped—the slave hunters weren't far away. A couple of hours at the most, he reckoned, and he would reach their camp.

Brimming with wrath and confidence, Nate set a

rapid pace. He felt no fear of the inky woods. The wilds were his home, after all.

But that didn't mean Nate became reckless. When a bear grunted nearby, he climbed a tree. Splashing told him the bear was in the river, after fish or frogs probably, or cavorting in bear fashion. He heard another grunt, and a mew, and was doubly glad he had climbed the tree.

It was a mother bear with a cub. No animal was more fiercely protective of her young. One whiff of his scent and she would tear down the tree to get at him.

Then Nate saw them, inky bulks with small shadows, wading the Platte. He stayed put until they reached the far side and disappeared into the undergrowth.

Descending, Nate took up his quest. He eagerly scanned the dark ahead, but there wasn't so much as a glimmer of orange.

By his reckoning an hour passed.

The possibility of being attacked was never far from Nate's mind. Twice something big crashed through the brush, and he crouched with his spear at the ready. In both instances, whatever it was ran off.

A second hour crawled on the footsteps of the first, and there was still no sign of a campfire. Apparently the slaver hunters were farther away than he thought.

Nate had a disturbing thought. What if they were *days* away? By the time he got to their camp, they would be long gone, well on their way to the Mississippi.

He would give anything for a horse.

The Big Dipper arced cross the sky until its position told him the time was close to midnight. He was sore and tired and hungry, but he wasn't about to stop this side of the grave.

"I'm coming, Winona."

To Nate's surprise, he got an answer: a bestial growl. Halting, he held his spear low in front of him, the sharpened tip angled up and out. He balanced on the balls of his feet, ready to lunge or spring aside.

Whatever growled was feline. Cat sounds were different from wolf and coyote sounds.

Gleaming emerald eyes confirmed his hunch. They were fixed on him with inhuman intensity. The size and shape could only be one animal: a cougar. A hungry cougar.

"Try and you die," Nate said.

A lot of animals ran at the sound of a human voice. Not this one. Snarling, it stalked closer.

Just what Nate needed. He stamped a foot and shouted, but it had no effect. He roared as a bear would roar, but the cat had figured out he wasn't a bear. He whooped. He whistled. He shrieked. In frustration he even tried a few cuss words.

A twig snapped to Nate's right, but he paid it no mind. He mustn't take his eyes off the cougar. The moment he broke eye contact, it could charge.

The vegetation on the other side of the trail rustled, and despite the cougar, Nate gave a quick look—and felt his blood change to ice.

A second pair of slanted eyes, nearly identical to the first, were peering back at him.

There wasn't just one cougar.

There were two.

Winona lay on her side facing the fire, pretending to be asleep. Her eyes were open a crack and she was watching Cranston. The nervous bundle of energy, as the whites would say, was standing watch. The rest of the slave hunters, as best she could tell, were asleep. As well they should be. As whites measured time, it had to be close to two in the morning.

Winona hoped the Worths were still awake. Before they lay down, she had whispered what she had in mind.

Samuel, in his eagerness to be free, had been all for it.

But not Emala. "Land sakes. Your plan could get us all killed. As bad as things are, I sure ain't anxious to breathe dirt."

"Not so loud," Samuel had cautioned.

"You can count me in, Mrs. King," Chickory said.

Randa, to Winona's surprise, hesitated. "I want to. I really and truly do. But you heard that man called Wesley. We give them trouble and they will hurt us."

"They can try," Samuel said. "Now that I've tasted freedom, I want more. I want to do as I please for the rest of my days."

Chickory said quietly, "I'm with you, Pa. Those men beat me. And the others laughed while they were doin' it. I hate them, Pa. I want to kill every last one."

"Now, now," Emala said. "What they did was bad. But if we start actin' like them, we're no better than they are."

"Maybe we aren't."

Emala twisted toward her husband. "Did you hear him, Samuel? Do you see what runnin' has brought down on our heads? Our own flesh and blood, talkin' as if I've never read him a lick of Scripture."

"What does the Bible have to do with this?" Samuel demanded.

"The Bible has to do with everything. It's God's

Word on how He wants us to be. Love thy neighbor. Turn the other cheek. Those are the rules we should live by."

"Are you insane? How can I love someone who is takin' me back to Georgia to hang? How can I turn the other cheek when all they'll do is hit me harder."

"Do you know what your problem is? You have no faith. Thank God I have enough for both of us."

Now, lying motionless, Winona looked from Wesley to Trumbo to the others. They appeared to be asleep. So too, to her dismay, did Randa and Chickory, who were on the other side of the fire. Winona couldn't tell about Samuel; he was behind her. Emala, though, had been opening her eyes every now and then, so she might be awake.

Cranston came over to the fire and held his hands out to the flames even though the night wasn't cold.

"If I was any more bored, I'd scream."

Winona took that as a good sign. He was more likely to doze off once he sat down—only he didn't sit down. He made another circuit of the clearing, muttering to himself. He might keep it up until he was relieved in a couple of hours.

Winona would rather deal with him than with the others. He didn't impress her as being nearly as vicious and dangerous as Olan and Wesley.

Her wrists and ankles were growing numb. She went to move them to restore the blood flow, and caught herself just in time.

She mustn't let Cranston know she was awake.

He came toward the fire.

Winona's hopes soared when he bent as if he were going to sit, but he only wanted to shake the coffeepot and see how much coffee was left. Replacing it, he sighed and strolled off toward the horses.

Winona decided to take a gamble. She was close enough to the fire to touch it. She thrust out her arms, and the flames engulfed her bound wrists. Terrible pain shot through her, but she grit her teeth and held her wrists steady for as long as she could stand it. Then, quickly drawing her arms back, she grit her teeth to keep from crying out.

The rope was smoldering, but it hadn't burned through.

Winona's wrists, on the other hand, were severely burned. Her skin was in agony. She made certain Cranston was still across the clearing, then went to do it again.

The whites of Emala's eyes shone in sheer horror. "Don't!" she whispered. "You'll hurt yourself worse!"

Winona did it anyway. The pain nearly caused her to black out. She half expected to be burned to the bone when she pulled her arms out of the flames. Only a few strands held the rope together. Gritting her teeth, she tugged and snapped them.

Winona examined her wrists. They were blistered and charred. But she was free, and that was the important thing. She checked on Cranston, wondering what was taking him so long. He was petting his horse!

Winona reminded herself that he was young yet, little more than a boy. But that wouldn't stop her from doing what she had to.

Feigning a light snore, Winona shifted so her knees were tucked high and her hands were at her ankles. She held her wrists together to give the impression they were still tied and pried at the knots on the rope around her ankles. "Keep an eye out," she whispered.

Emala nodded, fear in her wide eyes.

Winona thought of Nate; he should have been there by now. Something must have happened. From remarks dropped by her captors, it had to do with Peleg Harrod. The old frontiersman, it turned out, was working for Wesley. She wasn't surprised. She had instinctively distrusted him when she met him, and her instincts were seldom wrong.

The knots were resisting her attempts. Trumbo had done a good job.

Winona kept at it long after most would have given up. Her charred wrists weltered with pain, but long ago she had learned how to close her mind to discomfort and do what needed doing.

"*Psssst*," Emala whispered.

Winona glanced over. "What?" Just then, one of the knots came undone. She attacked the second.

"You asked me to keep watch."

Preoccupied with the ankle rope, Winona didn't understand what she was getting at. "You do not want to?"

"Dearie, I'd do just about anything for you. I just thought you'd want to know that he's coming back."

Winona shifted toward the horses.

Cranston was halfway to them.

Chapter Fourteen

The cougars were young, two from the same litter, Nate guessed, not yet ready to go their separate ways, hunting together. Because they were young, they were that much more dangerous. Older cougars were wary of humans. These two regarded him as no different than a deer or an antelope.

Swinging his spear back and forth, Nate sought to keep them at bay. Both slunk closer, snarling fiercely. He wondered which would come at him first.

Nate needed space to move, space to swing and thrust. He slowly backed away. Suddenly he bumped against a tree. He went to sidle around it, and the cougar on the right took a quick bound, cutting him off. He started to move to the left and the other cougar did the same. He was trapped between them with no way to turn.

Nate tried one more time. "Get out of here!" he bellowed. "Go eat something else!"

All the good it did him. Both cats crouched. Both growled. The cougar on the left started to stalk forward. A split second later, so did the cougar on the right.

Nate had fought mountain lions before. Lightning quick with razor claws and knife points for teeth, they were all sinew and ferocity. He would rather fight a bear than a mountain lion any day.

Their eyes gleamed eerily in the star shine. Their bodies were rigid, their tails stiff. They were focused on him and only him.

Nate eased into a crouch. He gave up the advantage of height to have a better advantage, which he demonstrated when the cougar on the left sprang. A living portrait of grace and power and savagery combined, it bared its fangs to rip and tear.

Pivoting, Nate drove the spear tip up and in. It caught the cat where its throat met its chest and sheared all the way through. The tree at Nate's back kept the sudden weight from bowling him over.

The cougar screeched once and went limp.

Nate shook his spear to get the cat off, but its body was caught fast. He turned toward the other one— and it was already in midair. Instantly, he did the only thing he could. He let go of the spear and grabbed the cat by the throat and one foreleg as it slammed into him. Again the tree kept him on his feet.

Hissing viciously, the cougar bit and clawed. Pain shot up Nate's arm. Flashing teeth narrowly missed his throat. Whirling, he slammed the cat against the trunk. Claws raked his side and he felt the moist sensation of blood.

What Nate wouldn't give for a gun or a knife.

He rammed the cat's head against the tree. He arced a knee into its ribs. He flung the cougar to the ground, but with the incredible agility of its kind, the cat landed on all fours and was at him again in the blink of a feline eye. It came at his legs and he kicked but it sprang nimbly out of reach.

Suddenly squatting, Nate scooped at the ground.

With a screech the cougar launched itself at him, and Nate threw dirt and grass into its face, into its eyes.

The cougar landed and scrambled away, blinking over and over, hissing in rage.

Nate had bought himself a few seconds. But his only weapon, the spear, was stuck fast in the other cat. He looked down, looked right and left, and then he looked up. A low branch was a foot above his head. He didn't hesitate. He jumped, gained a hold.

The cougar became a tawny streak.

Nate cried out. His pants were torn open. So was the flesh underneath. He tried to draw his legs up but the cat clung on, its claws buried. He kicked and lost his hold and fell. Fortunately the cougar let go and leaped to one side.

It came at him again and he punched at its face. Shrieking, the cat swung a claw-tipped paw.

Nate's sleeve felt wet with blood. He kicked again to keep the cougar away.

The beast crouched low to the ground, its tail swishing.

Nate swung at the same instant it leaped. His knuckles connected with its nose and the cat fell back, yowling. He braced for another attack, but it unexpectedly spun and bounded off into the inky undergrowth.

Nate stayed where he was. He half suspected the cougar would circle around and come at him from the other side. But the seconds became minutes, and it didn't reappear.

At last, convinced he had driven it off, Nate unfurled. He placed his foot on the dead cougar, gripped the spear with both hands, and pulled. Nothing happened. He tried again with the same result.

"Is it me or the spear?" Nate asked the empty air. Sitting, he propped one foot against the cat's chest and another against its throat and put all his weight and strength into wrenching the spear out. This time he succeeded, but the effort left him spent and breathing heavily. He wanted to lie back and rest, but an image of Winona filled his mind and heart with tender yearnings.

Nate got to his feet. The spear became a crutch. Turning eastward, he hiked as fast as he could. He became conscious of blood trickling down his hand and dripping from the tips of his fingers. He hitched at his sleeve, but it was too dark to tell how bad it was, except that some of the cuts were deep.

Dizziness washed over him. Stopping, he waited for the attack to pass. All around were the raucous sounds of the night. When he was strong enough he moved on.

The steady drip from his hand compelled him to seek the river. Kneeling on a gravel bar, he hiked his sleeve and plunged his forearm in the water. Of all his cuts, his arm was the worst. He figured to wash it and stop the bleeding and be on his way. He held his arm close to his face and saw that more blood was welling up. Stopping it would take some doing.

Desperate straits called for desperate measures. Nate roved the woods, gathering downed limbs and dry grass for kindling. Harrod had taken his guns and knife and tomahawk but not his possibles bag. Opening it, he took out his fire steel and flint.

Never in his whole life did it take Nate so long to start a fire. Finally sparks set the grass to burning and he puffed on the tiny flames. But they kept dying. Persistence paid off. Eventually he had a fire crackling. He rolled up his sleeve and examined the claw marks in the dancing light, and winced. He needed stitching but he couldn't do it himself.

Bunching his sleeve around his elbow, Nate grit his teeth and lowered his arm into the flames. The agony was awful. His flesh sizzled. The smell of blood filled the air. He almost blacked out but didn't. When he was sure he had stanched the flow, he staggered to the gravel bar and submerged his arm. Blessed coolness relieved some of the pain.

Nate didn't dally. He was thinking of Winona and the Worths. He looked up to get his bearings by the stars and was on his way. But he took only a few strides when more vertigo jumbled his equilibrium. Tottering, he clutched at a cottonwood, missed, and pitched onto his face.

"Winona," Nate breathed.

And passed out.

Winona King froze. She didn't think Cranston had noticed her moving, but she stayed perfectly still as he approached the fire. From under her eyelids she watched him refill his cup and sip coffee. He glanced in her direction.

"What are you looking at?"

For a few anxious seconds Winona thought he was talking to her. She was on the verge of replying when Emala answered him.

"I can't sleep."

"I don't care. Quit staring at me. Turn the other way or I'll come over there and kick your ribs in."

"Is it me or my skin you dislike so much?"

"I've never liked your kind. Your color, your hair—it's unnatural."

"And I suppose whites are fine?"

Cranston motioned at her with his cup. "White is better. White is smarter. White is stronger."

"Bosh, boy. My Samuel could break you in half without tryin'. There's not any of you as strong as my Samuel is except maybe that big one."

"Says you." Cranston turned his back on her. "I don't want any more of your jabber."

Winona got the last knot untied. She moved her legs to see if the blood had been cut off; they were fine.

"I never realized how much hate there is in this world," Emala said to the young slave hunter. "There's so much hate, if it was water, we'd all of us drown."

"The stupid things you say," Cranston said. "Now *quiet*, damn you. I won't tell you again."

Winona was on her feet and moving toward him before he finished speaking. He had a Green River knife in a sheath on his left hip. As silent as could be, she came up behind him, gripped the knife and eased it out. He felt the movement and his head snapped around just as she plunged the cold steel between his ribs. She knew just where to stab. She wasn't a warrior, but she had been taught by Touch the Clouds, her cousin and an esteemed Shoshone warrior.

In a situation like this, where her life hinged on the outcome, Touch the Clouds had advised her to go for the heart or the head. She went for the heart, and when the blade was all the way in, she twisted it. She would have sworn she felt his heartstrings tear.

Young Cranston's eyes grew wide, and he opened his mouth to scream but Winona clamped her other hand over it. He gurgled and stiffened. Fearing he would go into convulsions that would wake the rest of the slave hunters, she kicked his legs out from under him and lowered him to the ground.

Cranston died without another twitch or peep.

Winona glanced at the other whites, but none had stirred. She jerked the knife from Cranston's body and wet scarlet spurted over her fingers and wrist. His shirt was as good as anything to clean it on. Then she slid the blade into her own sheath. It fit fairly well.

Picking up the rifle, Winona also jammed one of his pistols under her belt. Being armed boosted her confidence. She backed up to where Emala lay and hunkered down to cut her free.

Emala was agog. "You . . . you . . . you."

"I took a life. It is them or us, and it will not be us."

"I could never do that. 'Thou shalt not kill.'"

Winona sliced the rope from Emala's wrists and then the rope around her ankles. "There," she whispered, and held the knife out to her, hilt first.

Emala scrunched up her face. "You want me to touch that? After you done got blood all over it?"

"I cleaned it."

"Not good enough."

"Would you rather die?" Winona shoved the hilt into Emala's hand. "Cut your husband and children free."

Shaking with revulsion, Emala sat up. "I never saw the like."

"You never saw anyone die before?"

"I never met a female like you. Ladies cook and sew and knit. They don't kill folks."

"Out here ladies do."

Emala started to say more, but Winona put a finger

to her lips. "We can talk about this later. We must get away while we can."

"Lordy. I am touching human blood."

"Hurry. Please."

Winona stood guard. It would be easy to put a slug into Wesley, but the others would swarm her before she could reload, and in their fury maybe kill the Worths as well as her.

Emala shook Samuel awake and cut him free. Then she crept to Randa, while Samuel moved to Chickory.

They had a tense moment when Olan muttered in his sleep and rolled onto his side. Bromley was snoring like a buffalo, puffing his long mustache with each exhale. Kleist had his blanket pulled up half over his blond hair.

Winona was surprised that Wesley hadn't woke up. Of all of them, she considered him the most dangerous, and she didn't take her eyes off him until Emala whispered her name and crooked a finger.

The Worths were hurrying to the horses.

Winona backed toward them. She didn't realize she had stepped in the pool of blood that ringed Cranston's body until her foot slipped out from under her and she nearly fell. It was amazing, how much blood the human body held. Going around, she dashed over.

Chickory was about to climb on.

"No!" Winona whispered. "We will lead them until we are far enough away that Wesley and his friends cannot hear us. And we will take the other horses with us."

Samuel showed his big teeth. "I like how you think. We'll strand them afoot. It will take them weeks to get back to civilization."

"Months," Winona amended.

"Just so we hurry," Emala urged, wringing her hands. "We can't be shed of these devils fast enough to make me happy."

Randa said, "We should kill them in their sleep."

"Hush, child," Emala scolded. "I won't have no daughter of mine stickin' folks like Mrs. King does."

"We could bash their heads in with rocks."

"Do you see any rocks handy?" Emala shook her head. "Let's just scat while the scattin' is good."

Winona was at her mare. She patted its neck and bent to cut the tether that linked the horses to one another.

A metallic *click* warned her they had run out of time.

Out of the darkness came Peleg Harrod, his rifle level. "Well, well, well. What do we have here?"

Chapter Fifteen

Nate King awoke to the dank scent of the earth in his nostrils. He remembered passing out. Fear filled him, fear he had been unconscious the whole night, but when he sat up he discovered, judging by the position of the Big Dipper, that it must be between three and four in the morning.

Nate slowly stood. He half expected another attack of dizziness, but he appeared to be fine. His arm hurt where he had cauterized the cuts but not that badly. Nearby lay his spear.

Then came a loud splash from the Platte River.

Nate turned, dreading it would be a bear. He almost laughed when he spied the silhouette of a doe in the act of crossing. On the shore beyond others waited for her.

"Enough wasting time," Nate said to himself, and began to hike east. Worry for his wife eclipsed all else. He must reach her without any more delays.

A growl from Nate's stomach reminded him he had not eaten anything since breakfast the morning before.

Passing out had done him some good. He wasn't as bone-tired as before. He was able to hold a fast pace. If he could keep the pace up, if he could spot their campfire, if he could reach their camp before daylight . . . if, if, if.

Nate thought of Harrod's betrayal, and what the man had put him through, and his blood boiled. He would like to get his hands on Harrod and vent his wrath.

The cool wind was a boon. He breathed deep and felt invigorated.

Now and again he flexed the fingers of his wounded arm to keep them from becoming stiff.

Minute by minute the night waned.

Dawn was an hour off and Nate was on the verge of bursting with frustration when in the distance, a finger of orange appeared. He stopped and rubbed his eyes and looked again. The pinpoint was still there. Eagerly, he pumped his long legs. He was so intent on the orange spot, he was oblivious to the woods around him until he came around a bend and the trail was blocked by a large bulk that snorted and reared from all fours onto its hind legs.

Nate stopped dead. It was another black bear. They weren't as fierce as grizzlies, but twice in his life he had nearly been killed by black bears and had learned to never, ever take them lightly. This one sniffed and cocked its head. A growl rumbled from its barrel chest.

Nate broke out in a sweat. This was the last thing he needed. He had the spear, but against a bear it was next to useless. He stayed still, his fate in the paws of the most unpredictable creature on God's green earth.

The bear took a lumbering step and did more sniffing.

Nate resisted an urge to run. Running from a bear sometimes incited them into attacking. Instead he looked the bear in the eyes and slowly raised his arms to make himself appear bigger.

The black bear's thin lips curled.

Nate firmed his hold on the spear. He wouldn't go down without a struggle. The bear's throat was its most vulnerable spot. A thrust to the jugular might prove fatal. If he could pierce the jugular, if he could avoid the enraged bear until it dropped . . . if, if, again.

There were too many if's in life.

The black bear lumbered closer. He saw saliva on the bear's teeth. He saw snot drip from its nose.

Just when Nate thought it would attack, the bear came down on all fours, and turned. A grunt and it was gone, melting into the vegetation with ghostly stealth.

Bears were crafty. Sometimes they lumbered off, only to circle around and come at their prey from another direction. Nate didn't linger. Holding his wounded arm to his side, he ran until his chest throbbed and his lungs were strained.

Slowing to a walk, Nate glanced back. The bear hadn't come after him. He gave silent thanks and moved on. The spot of orange was bigger. He was getting close.

Over and over in his head he repeated the same vow: *Winona is there. I must reach her. I must save her.* It became a chant, a litany.

Nate couldn't bear the idea of losing her. They had been together for decades. He didn't talk about it much because men didn't talk about such things, but she was the heart of his life.

He had a friend who believed that women were for cooking and sewing and cleaning, and for keeping men warm under the sheets. His friend's idea of love was a shallow stream watered by the runoff of need and not the deeper love that came from two hearts entwined.

Nate caught himself and shook his head in annoyance. Here he was thinking about love when he should be concentrating on one thing and one thing only. He raised his gaze to the orange. A quarter of a mile, he figured. And not much night left.

Nate walked faster. The slave hunters were bound to be up at the crack of dawn, and once awake, they would be that much harder to take by surprise.

"I'm coming, Winona."

The sound of his voice startled him. Maybe being alone in all that vastness had gotten to him.

When he was a couple hundred feet out, Nate slowed. He didn't want to; he had to. The crack of a twig could spoil everything. He moved with the care and patience of the Apaches he had tangled with years ago on a visit to Santa Fe.

The fire had burned low, which worked in his favor. The less light, the less likely they were to spot him before he was ready to be spotted.

At a hundred feet, Nate eased onto his belly and crawled. He wasn't taking any chances. Not with Winona's life at stake. And the lives of the Worths, of course.

Nate held the spear at his side and was careful it didn't snag. Never had he missed his rifle and pistols and bowie as much as he did right then. With guns he would have stood a good chance. Without them . . . He frowned and continued crawling.

Nate was a realist. He might come out on top. He might not. He thought of his son, Zach, and Zach's delightful spouse, Louisa. He thought of his best friend and mentor, Shakespeare McNair, and Shakeseare's Flathead wife, Blue Water Woman. He thought of happy times and happy memories, and made his peace. If it was to be, it was to be. When all was said and thought, a man, any man, or a woman, any woman, had no more control over their destinies than the guiding hand of the Almighty allowed.

Now Nate was close enough to hear the crackling of the flames. He was close enough to see that the ground around the fire was empty of sleeping forms. No one was there. Not the slave hunters. Not Winona. Not the Worths. Nor were there any horses.

They had gone, and left the fire burning.

Anger brought Nate to his feet. He charged into the clearing, his chest heavy with worry. Without a mount he had no hope of overtaking them. Fighting off despair, he shuffled to the fire. Near it was a dry pool of blood. He dropped the spear, sank to his knees, and said the name that meant more to him than anything. "Winona."

"She's right here, Injun lover."

Nate felt like the world's biggest fool. "You were waiting for me."

Six men ringed him with leveled rifles. One of the six was Peleg Harrod. "We were waiting for you, hoss. Let me introduce these other gents." He did so, ending with, "And this is the famous Grizzly Killer. Word has it he's killed more silver tips than any man alive."

"Want me to kill him, Wesley?" Trumbo asked. "A twitch of my finger and I'll splatter his brains."

The hawk-faced slave hunter cradled his Kentucky and came to the other side of the fire. "This was my doing. I don't like loose ends. I knew if I didn't finish it, you would track me down and hold me to account."

"You figured right." Nate peered into the dark. He was weary and worn and drained, and longed for one thing. "Where are they? What have you done with them?"

"Not a thing to the darkies. They're worth money. As for your squaw . . ." Wesley gestured at the dry blood. "There were seven of us, but she killed the boy standing watch. She shouldn't have done that. I was willing to do her quick, but now it won't be." He gestured again, at the encircling dark. "Fetch them. And don't forget the horses."

Harrod stayed where he was. "I'm right sorry about this, but money is money and he's paying me well."

"Judas was paid well, too."

Harrod jerked his head as if he had been slapped. "Hey now. I didn't kill you like I was supposed to. That should count for something."

Wesley faced the old frontiersman. "I've been meaning to talk to you about that, Peleg. We had an agreement, remember?"

"Of course."

"And you broke it."

"You have him, don't you?"

"That's not the point. You were to lead him back here into an ambush and we would kill him. With him dead, the rest would be easy to catch."

"It worked out, didn't it? The Worths and his woman rode right into your hands."

"It worked out, yes," Wesley said. "It worked out in spite of you not doing as I wanted."

Harrod mustered a grin. "You're not mad at me, are you?"

"I never get mad, Peleg. I never raise my voice. I never threaten. You should know that by now. I don't forgive, either. You should know that, too." Wesley's right hand rose, holding a flintlock. He thumbed back the hammer.

"Wait!" Harrod bleated.

"What for?"

"You can't kill me in cold blood."

"Why not? You've served your purpose."

"But you need me, remember. You need my experience."

"I needed you to help cross the prairie. But now we're heading back. I can manage right fine without you."

"You bastard. You just want to get out of paying me the rest of the money you owe me."

The pistol boomed and the back of the frontiersman's head exploded. Peleg Harrod's mouth fell open and his features went slack, and like so much mud he oozed into a heap and lay quivering.

Nate started to rise, but Wesley centered the Kentucky on him.

"I'd think twice, mountain man. But if you're in a hurry to die, you are welcome to try."

The others came running and stopped short at the sight of Harrod.

Olan laughed and slapped his thigh. "I never did like that old fart. Him and his airs about females."

"Fetch them," Wesley commanded, and when they hustled off, he turned to Nate. "Now it's your turn."

"Want me to turn my back to you to make it easy?"

"What I want is to know why," Wesley said.

"Why what?" Nate was watching for Winona. At that moment nothing else in the whole world mattered.

"Why did you help the blacks? What are they to you that you went to all this trouble?"

"We like them."

"That's all?"

"What else should there be?"

"I lost my best friend back in Missouri and had to trail you halfway across the plains, and all because you took a shine to a bunch of wooly heads?"

"They're our friends."

"Hell. You haven't known them that long. Yet you and your woman gambled your lives to save theirs." Wesley shook his head. "I'll never understand people like you."

"People who care for other people?"

"No. Whites who don't give a damn about their own color. You took a red wife and you made friends with these blacks. Don't you have any pride? Don't you have any dignity?"

"My wife could be any color under the sun and I would still be proud to be her husband." Nate was angered by the insult, and he fed on that anger for renewed vigor. "She's the finest woman I ever met."

"She's still a red squaw."

Nate balled his big fists and would have struck him if not for the unwavering muzzle of the Kentucky rifle.

"I suppose you don't believe in slavery, either?"

"Need you even ask?"

Wesley let out a long sigh. "One of those. You're from north of the Mason-Dixon, aren't you?"

"I was born and raised in New York."

"That explains it. You damn Yankees with your soft hearts. You cry and moan about how awful it is that we in the South lord it over blacks, and then you go and try to lord it over us by demanding we do as you want whether we want to or not, and set all the blacks free. You're a bunch of hypocrites."

"Making slaves of people is wrong."

"Slavery has been around since Bible times. It's nothing new."

Nate had more to say but just then the Worths were shoved and prodded into the firelight. Their hands were tied behind their backs. Samuel's ankles had been bound, as well, and the only way he could move was to hop like a rabbit.

Emala saw Nate, and sobbed.

"Where's Winona?"

"Your bitch is coming," Trumbo said.

Nate churned with fear. He scarcely breathed. When three figures came out of the dark he started to rise, but Wesley took a half step.

"Stay right where you are, mountain man."

Olan was on one side of Winona, Bromley on the other. She was as limp as a wet cloth, her long black hair hanging over her face.

"Here's your squaw," Olan said, and laughed.

They hurled Winona roughly to the ground and she rolled onto her back and was still.

Her hair fell from her face.

Nate looked, and thought he would scream.

Chapter Sixteen

They'd beaten her. They beat her about the face and head and neck, beat her so bad that every inch of skin was a bruise or a welt or a bump. Dry blood caked her chin and the corners of her mouth, and red ribbons were under her nose. They must have mashed her face in the dirt after they beat her because her wounds were smeared with it, and dirt was in her hair and speckled the top of her dress.

Deep within Nate King something snapped. He stared down at the woman he loved more than he loved anything or anyone, and it was as if an invisible hand reached into his chest, wrapped around his heart, and squeezed. A red-hot blaze of fury coursed through his veins and his temples throbbed to the beat of pure rage. He had thought he would scream, and now he did. But not a scream of anguish or despair. He screamed a scream of fury. He screamed in molten hate. He screamed as a man screams when all he is or was or ever will be lay hurt before his eyes. He screamed a scream ripped from the depths of his being.

Nate was up off his knees in a blur. The Kentucky boomed but he sidestepped and the slug missed. He drove his fist into Wesley's face with all the might of his iron muscles. Flesh pulped and teeth crunched, and Wesley went down, spitting blood. Still a blur, Nate whipped a backhand that caught Olan across the jaw and sent him tumbling. A pistol cracked, Bromley this time, but again the shot missed. Nate kicked him in the groin, and it was as if a hog squealed at its own slaughter.

Then Trumbo pounced, closing from behind and wrapping his huge arms around Nate's. "I've got him!"

Nate rammed his head back and cartilage gave way with a wet *splat*. Trumbo grunted, and his grip slackened. With a powerful heave, Nate broke free and whirled. Trumbo reached for him, but Nate launched an uppercut that started at his knee and lifted Trumbo onto his heels and sent him crashing to the earth.

That left the blond man, the one called Kleist. He had wisely stayed back and now he took aim with a pistol, thinking he had the time.

Nate bent and grabbed the unlit end of a burning brand from the fire and threw it at Kleist's face. Kleist did what anyone would do—he ducked. It gave Nate the second he needed to take a long bound and drive his fist deep into the blond man's gut.

All the men were down, some not moving, some thrashing and cursing and spitting.

Nate had eyes only for Winona. He dashed to her side and gently lifted her. The sight of her battered, bloodied face so close to his caused another cry to be torn from his innermost being, and then he was racing for the trees with her clutched protectively to his broad chest.

"Stop him, damn it!" Wesley bellowed. "Shoot him, someone!"

Someone tried. A pistol blasted and lead buzzed by Nate's ear. A few more strides and he was in heavy cover. He kept running. He ran and ran until his sides were heaving. Caked with sweat, filled with dread, he stopped in a clear space and lowered Winona onto her back.

"Oh, God."

Nate fought down another cry. He touched her cheek, which was crisscrossed with welts and terribly swollen, and his eyes moistened.

"If they've killed you . . ."

Nate couldn't finish. He clasped her wrist and felt for a pulse and nearly whooped for joy when he found one, strong and regular. He pressed an ear to her bosom to listen to her heart.

"Thank you, thank you, thank you, thank you."

Swallowing to rid his throat of a lump, Nate raised his head. He had lost all sense of direction. The North Star gave him the clue he needed. Apparently he was east of the slave hunters' camp. Which meant the river should be to his left.

Picking up Winona again with the utmost care, Nate carried her to a grassy flat at the water's edge.

"Please," Nate said. He cupped his hand and dribbled water on her face and neck. She groaned, and stirred. He kissed her, then dipped his hand in again and trickled drops between her parted lips and down her throat.

Winona coughed and blinked, and her swollen mouth curled in a hint of a smile. "Are you trying to drown me, Husband?"

"Thank the Lord."

Winona coughed some more and went to turn her head, and winced. "I take it you saved me?"

Nate couldn't talk for the new lump in his throat, so he nodded.

"You were a bit late this time."

Nate bowed his forehead to her shoulder and sobbed. He held her sides and trembled.

"Husband?" Winona had never seen him like this, not in all the years of their togetherness.

"I thought—" Nate said, and couldn't finish.

"Oh, sweet one." Winona ran her fingers through his black mane. "I am here and I am alive. Be strong."

Nate nodded. Sniffling, he sat up and wiped his face with a sleeve. "If I ever did lose you, I wouldn't be able to go on living."

"Husband!" Winona said again, and winced again, as well. "I sure do hurt. I killed one of them and they were mad. They beat me, Olan and that Bromley and the German, Kleist."

"Not Wesley or Trumbo?"

"No. They stood and watched, and Wesley said not to kill me, that I was bait to bring you, and they must keep me alive until I served my purpose."

"They're all going to die."

Winona rose onto her elbows and squinted through puffy eyes. "The Worths, Grizzly Killer? Where are they?"

"The slave hunters have them. I couldn't save them *and* you. I was unarmed and it was five to one."

"We cannot abandon them."

"Do you honestly think I would?"

Nate cradled her head in his lap and caressed her hair and said softly, "I went berserk. The very thing I have warned Zach about time and again."

"Where do you think he got it from? He is more

like you than he is willing to admit." Winona grasped his hand and closed her eyes. "Tell me. Do I look as terrible as I feel?"

"You would scare infants."

Winona started to laugh but stopped. "Don't do that, Husband. It hurts too much."

"I love you."

"I love you, too."

For a while they lightly touched and lightly kissed and then Winona said, "And you were right, Husband."

"About what?"

"They must die. Especially the one who hurt me the most, that Olan. I will cut out his heart while he is still alive and show it to him as he dies."

"Only if you get to him before I do."

In all his born days Samuel Worth had never seen the like. The mountain man had torn through the slave hunters like a tornado through a cotton field. Samuel yearned to have fought at Nate's side, but bound as he was, all he could do was lie helpless with frustration and give a whoop of joy when Nate made it into the woods with Winona in his arms.

"Lordy!" Emala exclaimed. She had seen it but couldn't believe it. That one man could do all that. As near as she could tell, he got away without a scratch. The hand of Providence, she decided, and gave inward thanks.

Chickory was speechless with amazement. He had seen only a few violent acts, and none were like this. It reminded him of the Bible stories his ma used to read to him. Stories in which Samson or David or Joshua would smite their enemies, hip and thigh.

Randa was glad Mr. and Mrs. King got away. Now she was worried for her parents and her brother. The slave hunters were in a foul mood. They had recovered and a few were on their feet. They looked fit to kill anyone who glanced at them crosswise.

Olan swore and continued swearing until Wesley snapped at him in anger.

"Enough, damn you. All he did was wallop you on the jaw." Wesley spat blood and bits of broken teeth.

Trumbo had a huge hand over the center of his face. "I've got a busted nose, Wes. I can hardly breathe."

"Breathe through your mouth then."

"Oh. I forgot. Thanks."

Bromley sat up, his hands over his crotch. "That son of a bitch. He about ruined me for women."

"He's a panther, that one," Kleist said. "The next time we run into him, we'll shoot him on sight."

Olan said, "We've seen the last of him and good riddance. Now that he's got his woman, he'll leave us be."

"No, he won't," Wesley said, scarlet leaking from a corner of his mouth. "He'll be back. Him and his sqaw both." He nodded at the Worths. "We have something they want."

"That's right!" Olan declared, and brightened. "Do you know what this means? We can set a trap for them. See to it his mouth-and nose-busting days are over."

"He won't be easy," Kleist remarked.

"He broke my nose," Trumbo said.

Wesley pressed ran a hand across his bloody mouth. "Olan's right. We need to figure out how to draw them in, and we need to do it right."

"We did it right the first time," Bromley said.

"Tell that to my mouth."

Emala cleared her throat. "If you don't mind, Mr. Wesley, sir, I have something to say."

"You have nerve, darkie. Keep it short. I'm not in the mood for any of your simpleminded shenanigans."

"Don't call her that," Samuel said.

"Which? Darkie? Or simpleminded? Not that it matters. She's both. And I'll call her whatever I damn well please."

"Don't bicker over me," Emala said quickly, to spare Samuel a possible beating. To Wesley she said, "I don't want any harm to come to the Kings on our account."

"You don't, huh?"

"No. So how about if we leave them a message?" Emala proposed. "You got any paper in those packs? And somethin' I can write with? I'll say they should go on to the mountains and leave us in God's hands."

Samuel said sharply, "You'll do no such thing, woman, you hear?"

"It's for their sakes," Emala said.

Wesley thoughtfully regarded her. "You really think they would do as you ask?"

"They've become good friends these past weeks. They'll do as I ask if I ask real nice."

Now it was Olan who objected. "Don't listen to her. We *want* the Kings to come after us so we can pay that big bastard back for what he did to us."

"Next time you might get more than a bop on the jaw," Emala warned. "Did you think of that?"

"I ain't scared of Nate King," Olan boasted.

"Then you're a fool."

"That mountain man is a hellacious fighter," Trumbo said.

Emala stared at Wesley. "So, what will you do? Will you or won't you let me?"

Wesley came and stood over her. "Oh, you'll get to write Nate King a note, all right. But it won't be what you were going to write. You'll say what I tell you."

"What would that be?"

"You'll beg King and his squaw to help you. You'll say you're afraid of what will happen to your husband when we get him back to the plantation. You'll say the Kings are your only hope, and to come quick."

"I'll do no such thing."

Wesley pointed his rifle at Chickory and put his thumb on the hammer. "You'll do it or you'll be shy a son."

"We're worth more money to you alive," Emala countered. "You said so yourself."

"Money I can't spend if I'm dead." Wesley pressed the muzzle to Chickory's temple, and Chickory flinched. "I'll gladly give up some of it to be sure I live to collect the rest."

Emala stared at her son and then at the rifle and then at the slave hunter holding it. "You're a vile man."

"Is that a no?"

"Don't shoot. I'll write your note, but I'll hate every word you make me say." Emala's eyes moistened.

Wesley motioned to Trumbo. "Go look in the packs for the paper."

"What I want to know," Olan said, "is how you aim to get this note to Nate King? It's not as if we know where to find him."

"We don't have to. He'll come to us." Wesley

walked to the center of the clearing. "We'll pound a stick in the ground right here. We'll split one end and put the note in it. King will come along, read it, and light out after us hell-bent to rip out our guts."

"What good does that do us?" Olan asked.

"Don't you see? We'll find a perfect spot for an ambush, and he'll be so fired up to save the darkies, he'll waltz right into our guns' sights."

"I like it," Olan said. "I like it a lot."

"I pray to God that Nate doesn't fall for it," Emala said.

"Quit with the God talk, woman," Olan said. "I don't believe in that stuff. There's no God Almighty and there's no hereafter. As Nate King and his wife will find out soon enough."

Chapter Seventeen

They jogged tirelessly for hours. They were both in superb condition, but Winona had to stop now and again. Once, she apologized, saying, "I am sorry, Husband. The pain."

"You're holding up fine."

Nate would wait, Winona would nod, and they would set out again.

They weren't near the Platte. They weren't in the woods that bordered it. They were at the edge of the prairie where the going was easy and they could cover a lot of ground quickly. They had a lot of ground to cover.

"I hope this works," Winona said between deep breaths. "I do not want to go to all this trouble for nothing."

"It's the last thing they'll expect."

On they jogged, through the heat of the morning and the haze of the afternoon. They stopped to rest only once, at midday. Making their way to the river, they lay on their bellies and stuck their sweat-slick faces in the water.

"Oh, my. This feels so nice, Husband. You rest on the bank. I will pretend I am a fish."

Rolling onto his side, Nate watched her dip her

head back in. He reached over and lightly touched her shoulder, whispering, "If you only knew how much . . ." Then, easing onto his back, Nate laced his fingers under his head and exhaled a long, tired sigh.

Bright blue painted the vault of sky save for a few fluffy white clouds. A finch flew past, a spot of yellow dwarfed by the blazing yellow higher up. Nate started to close his eyes but snapped them open again.

Winona came up for air, and grinned. "I used to do this a lot when I was little."

"You're weird."

Winona laughed, then stiffened and pushed up on her hands. "Did you hear something?"

"No. Relax. We're well ahead of them by now."

"I hope so."

"I know so. I checked the ground. If they'd already passed, there would be fresh tracks."

Gaining her knees, Winona turned. "I would be more confident if we had guns."

"We have these," Nate said, and tapped his temple. "Guns or not, when it happens it will be fast and brutal."

"Killing usually is." Winona lay next to him. She ran a finger over a welt. "This is one time I will not mind. Were my mother still alive, she would be upset with me."

"For wanting revenge on the men who did that?"

"Morning Dew had a gentle heart. She would fight when she had to, as the time our village was raided and when those Blackfeet attacked us. But she did not like violence. When my father talked about counting coup, she would say he had no need to prove he had courage. She knew he did."

"What did your father say?"

"Black Kettle always smiled and told her that he didn't count coup for her, he did it to protect our people."

"I liked your father and mother."

"They liked you."

For a while they were quiet. Then Nate grunted and sat up. "Enough rest. We have to keep going. I figure we're a mile and a half ahead of them by now. By nightfall I'd like to be three or four."

"I am not an Apache, Husband. I cannot run forever."

"If you tire, I'll carry you." Nate bent and offered her his hand. As he pulled her to her feet she came into his arms and kissed him on the neck. "What was that for?"

"When two hearts are one, neither heart needs a reason."

They stood in silent embrace, his chin on her head, until the chirp of a robin brought them back to the here and now.

"When we get home I am barring our cabin door and we are not stirring out of bed for a week."

"I'll hold you to that," Nate said, and gave her a playful smack on her bottom.

They hiked to the edge of the prairie and resumed jogging. Minute after minute, hour after hour. They saw deer and elk. They saw rabbits and squirrels. They spied a few buffalo far out on the plain. Once they spotted a young black bear that ran off when it spotted them.

"Now that's the kind of bear I like," Nate said.

As the afternoon waned, Nate stopped frequently so Winona could catch her breath. She protested that she was holding him up and he merely smiled.

Nate could hardly stand to look at her bruised

and swollen face. Hate festered in him, and he was not a hating man. The slave hunters deserved what he was going to do to them.

The sun was less than an hour shy of setting when Nate announced, "This is far enough!" He came to a stop.

Winona, puffing, doubled over with her hands on her hips. "I thought you wanted to keep going until sunset."

Nate glanced at her heaving sides and the sweat dripping from her brow. "We've been at this most of the day and I'm wore out."

With masterly sarcasm Winona said, "Oh, really?" She took hold of his hand and grinned. "Always tell the truth, Husband. You are stopping because you are worried about me."

"We have a long night ahead of us."

They went to the river, rested, drank and set to work. First they waded into the shallows and scoured the bottom for fist-sized flat stones with thin edges. These they chipped and sharpened with other stones. Then they went in among the trees, searching.

The digging was the hard part. Their palms blistered and hurt, but they kept at it, taking turns, until the job was done.

The night filled with the cries and shrieks of predator and prey, but the meat eaters left them alone.

It was pushing four in the morning, by Nate's reckoning, when he stepped back and nodded in grim satisfaction. "This will have to do."

"Limbs instead of rope," Winona said. "I hope they work."

"Whether they do or they don't, there will be a reckoning."

* * *

Samuel Worth squinted against the harsh glare of the sun and licked his dry, cracked lips. He had been tied to a stake for most of the day and his body was burning hot. Beads of sweat trickled down his brow and into his eyes and made them sting. For the umpteenth time Samuel strained against the stakes his wrists and ankles were tied to, but the stakes didn't give. He glanced to the right at his wife and then to the left at his daughter and his son, and he summed up how he felt with, "Damn me to hell."

Emala opened her eyes. "What have I told you about cussin' in front of the children?"

"I'm not no child, Ma," Chickory said.

"Me either," said Randa.

The brush rustled and out strode Olan. "If the four of you don't shut the hell up, I will damn well shut you up."

"The whole world is cuss crazy," Emala said.

There was more rustling and the others came out of hiding: big, bearded Trumbo; Bromley with his shotgun; Kleist, the German; and, last of all, Wesley. The backwoodsman glanced skyward and frowned.

"Another hour and the sun will set."

"I don't understand it," Trumbo rumbled. "Where are the Kings? We were so sure they'd come after these darkies."

"We're people, just like you," Samuel told him. "We have names, just like you."

Olan uttered a cold laugh. "Will you listen to him? The airs he puts on." He took a step and kicked Samuel in the ribs as hard as he could. "When will you get it through your stupid head that we don't care? To me you're the same as dogs."

Agony gripped Samuel and wouldn't let go. He tried to double over but couldn't, staked out as he was. Gasping for breath, he shook from head to toe. At least one of his ribs was busted, he was sure.

Emala's eyes filled with tears and she choked down a sob. "Leave him be, you hear? He never did anything to you for you to treat him like that."

"He's black. That's all it takes."

"Enough," Wesley said. He moved past the Worths and gazed down the trail to the west. "This bothers me. It bothers me something fierce."

"What?" Kleist asked.

"Yeah, what?" Trumbo echoed.

"The Kings. They're not the kind to let this drop. They should have been here by now. They should have read the note and come on fast." Wesley gestured at the Worths. "I figured they'd spot these four staked out and lose their caution, and we'd have them."

Emala chortled. "Nate King ain't no fool. He'd know it was a trap and hold back until dark."

"Could be." Wesley pointed at Trumbo and Kleist. "I want the two of you to backtrack half a mile or so. Do it careful. Look for sign of the mountain man and his squaw."

"We'll fetch our horses." Trumbo went to turn.

"Did I say to ride?" Wesley snapped. "Go on foot. That way you won't leave sign telling King we're expecting him."

"Oh. You're right. I didn't think again."

"That's what I'm for." Wesley turned and squatted next to Samuel. "Your wrists and ankles are bleeding. I told you not to try to get free, but you didn't listen."

"What do you care?"

"Not a damn bit. But I have a job to do and it helps me do the job faster and easier if you're not weak from loss of blood." Wesley regarded him thought-fully. "Your woman says that you and the Kings are friends. Is that true?"

Samuel had to fight the pain to say, "I expect as we are now, yes. Why do you want to know?"

Emala piped up with, "They like us so much, they've invited us to come live in their valley."

"This bothers me more and more. If they like you so damn much, where the hell are they?" Wesley rose. "We'll spend the night here. If the Kings don't show by morning, we'll head out."

Samuel thought of the suffering his wife and children would go through. "You're not goin' to keep us staked out like this all night, are you?"

"No." Wesley drew his knife and cut a strip from Samuel's shirt. "Open your mouth."

"I'll be damned if I will."

Wesley jabbed the tip of the blade against Samuel's neck. "You think you can sass me because I want you alive for the money. But there's nothing that says I can't chop off a finger or toe. Or how about if I feed you your daughter's nose or an ear?"

"I hate you," Samuel said. But he opened his mouth. His piece of shirt tasted of sweat.

"Why didn't we gag them earlier?" Olan asked. "They'd have yelled their heads off to warn the Kings."

"That they would," Wesley agreed. "All of them, all at the same time, making so much noise, the Kings wouldn't hear us close in for the kill."

Olan chuckled. "Trumbo is always saying about how you're as slick as axle grease, and I have to agree. Could be I'd like to work with you steady if you can give me your word my poke won't ever go empty."

"Equal shares is how we split the bounties. Not many runaways are worth as much as this bunch. But I've never had less than a hundred dollars in my poke in all the years I've been chasing black sheep."

Emala had put up with all she was going to. "We're not sheep! We're human beings!"

Wesley leaned down and pinched the fleshy part of her upper arm so hard, she cried out. "It riles me when your kind claim to be the same as me. Take a good look, cow. I'm human, and my skin is white. Your skin is black. That makes you something else."

"How can you think that? How can you be so twisted inside?"

"You just can't stand to hear the truth, you lump of ugliness." Wesley cut a strip from her dress and bunched it up. "Open wide."

Emala couldn't say what made her do it. When he started to stuff the gag between her teeth, she bit down with all her might. Blood spurted and bone crunched. She swallowed some of the blood and nearly gagged.

Suddenly Olan was there. The stock of his rifle rose and fell.

"Emala!" Samuel cried.

"Ma!" Randa wailed.

Chickory was dumbstruck with horror.

Wesley clutched his hand, grit his teeth and hissed, "The bitch! The miserable bitch!" He pressed his bleeding finger to his side and grimaced. "First my teeth. Now this."

Samuel stared aghast at the blood trickling from his wife's brow. "If you've busted her skull, so help me—"

"As thick as her head is?" Olan responded, and laughed. "Hell, I'm lucky I didn't bust my rifle."

"In all the years I've been at this," Wesley said, "no runaways have ever given me as much trouble. And I have a feeling the worst is yet to come."

"The mountain man?"

"And his squaw. Don't forget her."

"She's female, for God's sake."

"She's a red savage, and she will kill if she has to." Wesley gazed to the west. "As surely as anything, they'll try to stop us. I don't know when and I can't say how, but they will."

"Let them. Nate King won't be so lucky next time." Olan fingered the hilt of his knife. "Me, I'm looking forward to making a tobacco pouch out of his wife's hide."

Chapter Eighteen

A bee buzzed past Emala and she gave a slight start. Ordinarily she would be near panic. Bee stings hurt like the dickens and made her puff up something awful. But she was too upset to panic. Her world had come crashing down around her. Not only that, her head was pounding. Not as bad as the night before but bad enough that she could hardly think.

The slave hunters were strung out in a line. Bromley was in the lead, his shotgun across his saddle. Next came Wesley and Trumbo. Kleist was leading the Worths' mounts. Last came Olan, in charge of the packhorse, whistling to himself.

For the hundredth time Emala tested the rope that bound her wrists. It was as tight as ever. She bit off a cuss word. She didn't believe in swearing, and she was doing her best to convince Samuel not to, but Samuel was a man and men had been put on earth to try female patience.

"Lord, preserve us," Emala breathed.

"What did you say?" Samuel twisted around. "Are you all right? How are you holdin' up?"

Emala couldn't get over how devoted he had acted all day. He hung on her every word and was always asking how she was doing. It made her suspicious.

When men are nice, they have a secret reason. "I'm fine," she fibbed. "But thank you for askin'." If he could be polite, so could she.

They neared a bend in the Platte. The river, usually shallow, deepened and widened into a series of pools. Finches and sparrows chirped in the brush. Warblers sang high in the trees. Squirrels scampered from limb to limb, and a long-eared rabbit bounded off. Does pricked their ears and fled with their white tails erect. In one of the pools a large beaver swam toward a mound of sticks.

Emala couldn't get over it all. So many creatures, it was the Garden of Eden all over again. It was strange how things worked out, she reflected. Here she had been dragged against her will from her life as a slave, only to find Samuel had been right and being a slave was no life at all. She wouldn't ever admit it, but she loved being free, loved it more than anything except her children and possibly Samuel.

And just when Emala was starting to savor the joy of being alive, along came the slave hunters and their hired killers to drag her and hers back to the life she despised.

Life just wasn't fair.

"No, it sure ain't," Samuel declared.

Emala realized she had spoken aloud.

"If only we'd made it to the mountains, they'd never have found us. We'd be free forever."

Wesley slowed and waited for Samuel to come up alongside him. "I heard that. The price on your heads, you'd have hunters after you from now until you're six feet under."

"Surely they wouldn't follow us all the way to the Rocky Mountains?" Emala said, surprised.

"How long before it sinks in? Five thousand dollars is more than most men make in ten years."

They started around the bend. Trees hid the next stretch of trail. Emala was surprised when Wesley suddenly drew rein and rose in the stirrups. She was even more surprised when she saw why.

Bromley and Trumbo had stopped. They had to.

The trail ahead was blocked. A pine tree had fallen across it. That wasn't unusual. Trees were felled all the time by high winds or heavy rain or simple age.

"Go around," Wesley commanded.

Bromley nodded and jabbed his heels. To the left of the fallen tree were briars, so he reined to the right to pass between the downed tree and a stand of saplings. There was a loud *crunch*, as if his horse had stepped on a branch, and a sapling whipped up off the ground with a whoosh. Bromley saw it and tried to dodge but he was too slow.

Emala was flabbergasted by what happened next.

One of the sapling's limbs had been trimmed and sharpened to a point. The tip lanced into Bromley's left side, and he cried out. Then the sapling whipped back again, pulling Bromley with it. The spear jerked free, spraying blood, and Bromley sprawled onto the ground and clutched at the spurting hole.

"Help him!" Wesley roared.

Trumbo, stunned, recovered his wits and swung down. He dashed to Bromley, who was flopping wildly about and swearing like a madman. Trumbo grabbed Bromley's shoulder, but Bromley pushed his hand away and went on thrashing.

"Oh, God! Not like this! Don't let it be like this!"

Wesley and the others swung down. Kleist dashed over to Trumbo, yelling at Bromley, "Lie still so we can see how bad it is!"

Emala never liked the sight of blood. So much was pumping from Bromley, it about made her sick. But God help her, she couldn't look away.

Trumbo and Kleist both got hold of Bromley just as he arched his head to the sky, let out a strangled gasp and went limp.

"Bromley?" Kleist said, and shook him. He put his ear to the bloody shirt and then felt for a pulse. "He's dead!"

"There must be redskins hereabouts," Trumbo declared.

Wesley went over to the sapling and stared at the blood dripping from the sharpened limb. "Injuns, hell. This is Nate King's doing. His and that squaw of his."

"But how?" Trumbo said. "They're on foot and we have horses. How'd they get ahead of us?"

"Only one way they could have," Wesley surmised. "They didn't stop at night like we did."

Olan pushed Trumbo aside and knelt next to Bromley. "Damn them to hell. Brom and me were pards for years."

"We need to bury him," Kleist said.

Wesley shook his head. "Like hell. That could be just what the Kings want us to do. Let down our guard so they can jump us. Take Bromley's shotgun and his knife and whatever else is worth taking and we'll light a shuck."

"You just hold on," Olan said. "He was our pard. We owe it to him to plant him so the critters don't feed on his remains."

"Maybe you want them to feed on yours?"

"Are you threatening me?"

"I'm reminding you." Wesley motioned at the woods. *"The Kings are out there."*

Olan and Kleist and Trumbo all trained their rifles on the greenery, and the latter rumbled deep in his barrel chest, "We should go in after them."

"And have them pick you off before you get ten feet? No." Wesley hefted his rifle. "Do as I told you."

They continued east, Kleist out in front, Olan once more at the rear, leading Bromley's mount and the pack animals. Presently they came to another bend.

Emala was watching ducks out on the water. She didn't realize those in front of her had halted until her own horse stopped. "I'll be!" she exclaimed.

Another pine tree lay across the trail. To the left was the river bank, to the right high grass.

"That tree didn't fall by itself," Trumbo said.

"You're learning," Wesley said. "We won't fall for the same trick twice. Swing to the left along the bank and stay shy of the trees."

Kleist nodded and reined to the left. His dun stepped on the bank—and the bank gave way. There were loud snapping sounds, and the earth caved in. The sharpened ends of stout branches came poking out. The dun squealed. Kleist, with remarkable agility, threw himself clear of the falling horse. He rolled and landed with a huge splash on his back in the water.

That the bank had collapsed startled Emala no end. She realized someone had dug it out and rigged sections of sod over a frame of tree branches so the bank appeared solid when it wasn't.

The dun was trying to stand but couldn't; it had been impaled by several of the branches.

Kleist lay in the water half submerged, his eyes wide, his mouth moving but no words coming out.

"What in the world?" Emala said. Then she saw the sharpened ends of stakes sticking through his chest and belly. The stakes had been imbedded in the bottom below the bank.

"Kleist!" Olan roared, and raced past the Worths.

"Watch out!" Wesley shouted. "The Kings might be nearby!"

They were.

Nate and Winona were flat on their bellies on the other side of the downed pine. Nate cautiously rose partway, a spear in each hand. He peered over the pine and saw Olan vaulting down the collapsed bank to get to Kleist. Wesley and Trumbo were still on their horses.

Ducking, Nate nodded at Winona and whispered, "It worked. There are three of them left. Here we go." Staying low, he ran to the end of the downed pine farthest from the river.

Winona was a step behind him. She held shorter spears, their ends sharpened and hardened in a fire.

Nate didn't slow. He swept around the end of the tree and flew toward the nearest rider, who happened to be Trumbo. The bearded bear didn't hear him until Nate was almost on top of him.

Bellowing in alarm, Trumbo spun in the saddle and went to bring up his rifle.

Nate drove one of his spears up and in. It was like stabbing into clay. Trumbo grunted and grabbed the spear, and Nate let go. Whirling, he streaked toward Wesley.

Winona veered to attack Olan. He was almost to Kleist, yelling Kleist's name over and over. As for Kleist, he wasn't moving; his blood was staining the water dark.

Winona came to the edge of the bank and launched herself into the air.

"Olan! Behind you!" Wesley shouted.

Olan turned just as Winona slammed into him. She stabbed at his chest, but somehow she missed. They tumbled and rolled in the river. Instantly, she was up, both spears ready. Olan had lost his rifle, but he came up clawing for a pistol.

Nate's eyes were locked on Wesley like an eagle's on prey. He resisted an impulse to see how his wife was doing and cocked his arm. He was only four or five feet from Wesley's horse when Wesley whipped around, leveled his Kentucky and fired from the hip. Nate felt a burning sensation, and then he was close enough. He thrust up and in, as he had done with Trumbo. But where Trumbo was big and slow, Wesley was sinewy and lightning-quick. Wesley twisted aside and swung the rifle stock at Nate's head. Dodging, Nate grabbed the rifle and wrenched it with all his strength.

Wesley let go, but now he was half-on and half-off his horse, with only one foot in a stirrup. He snatched at his waist and jerked the flintlock clear.

Nate had a spear in one hand and the Kentucky rifle in the other. He swung the rifle, clubbing Wesley's forearm, and Wesley's lost hold of the pistol. Dropping the rifle, Nate seized Wesley's shirt and unhorsed him, slamming him down hard. A foot caught Nate in the gut. Nate drew back and raised the spear, but another kick racked his knee with pain and his leg nearly buckled.

Over in the water, Winona stabbed Olan in the hand. He howled with rage as the flintlock plopped into the water, and then he backpedaled, cursing her fiercely. She went after him, stabbing with both spears again and again. She caught him in the shoulder. Another thrust drew blood from his thigh.

Baring his teeth, Olan growled like an animal and resorted to his knife. "I'll kill you, bitch! Kill you! Kill you!" He was on her in a rush.

Nate saw his wife's mortal struggle out of the corner of his eye, but he couldn't go to her aid. He had his own situation to deal with. Wesley had regained his feet and pulled a tomahawk from behind his back.

It was Nate's tomahawk, the one the slave hunters took from him days before.

Wesley crouched, snarling, "You've been a thorn in my side long enough."

Nate didn't respond. He parried with the spear, shifted, countered a swing that would have cleaved his head like a melon. Wesley was grinning, the epitome of confidence and raw vitality. Nate barely avoided having his thigh opened. They circled, eyeing each other, each waiting for the other to strike.

Nate had his back to the river. He heard Olan curse, and loud splashing. Wesley glanced past him, and his grin widened.

"Your squaw is dead, and you're next."

God help him, Nate had to look. It was Winona, the woman he loved, the woman who was his heart made flesh. He looked and froze in dismay.

Winona and Olan were down, locked together, roiling the water, the tip of Olan's knife inches from her throat.

"Mr. King!" Emala screamed.

Nate jerked back, not sure where the blow was coming from. The razor edge of the tomahawk flashed past his eyes, so close that it nicked the bridge of his nose. He thrust hard and true, his spear penetrating just below Wesley's jaw and going completely through and out the other side.

Wesley gripped the spear and staggered. He tried to say something, but all that came from his mouth, and his nose besides, was blood and more blood. The tomahawk fell.

Grabbing it, Nate whirled and raced for the river.

Winona was on her back, struggling to keep her face above the surface. She couldn't see Olan well because of the water in her eyes, and she could scarcely catch her breath because of the water in her mouth and throat. She tried to hold on to Olan's wrist so he couldn't stab her but he suddenly tore free. Winona blinked, and cold steel gleamed high.

"I've got you now, you bitch!"

There was another gleam, above Olan. Before his knife could descend, the second gleam arced down, and Olan's face did an amazing thing: It split in half, from the crown to the chin, one eyeball and one cheek going one way and the other eyeball and cheek the opposite way. From out of the cleft oozed blood and brains, and more.

Nate grabbed the back of Olan's shirt and flung him away. Bending, he hooked his arm under Winona and levered her to her feet. Stricken with fear, he looked for wounds but saw none. "Are you all right?"

"I am now."

"I thought—"

"Thank you."

They embraced. Nate breathed deeply of her scent. Winona had a lump in her throat.

Samuel ran over, gnawing at the rope around his wrists. "You did it!" he happily exclaimed. "They're by God dead!"

Randa and Chickory were close behind, Emala slower.

"What have I told you about takin' the Almighty in vain? Land sakes, men are thickheaded."

Nate turned and held out his tomahawk. "Here. Let me cut you free."

Emala stared at the carnage and shuddered. "Lordy. This wilderness is goin' to take some gettin' used to."

ROBERT J. CONLEY

FIRST TIME IN PRINT!

No Need for a Gunfighter

"One of the most underrated and overlooked writers of our time, as well as the most skilled."
—Don Coldsmith, Author of the Spanish Bit Saga

BARJACK VS...EVERYBODY!

The town of Asininity didn't think they needed a tough-as-nails former gunfighter for a lawman anymore, so they tried—as nicely as they could—to fire Barjack. But Barjack likes the job, and he's not about to move on. With the dirt he knows about some pretty influential folks, there's no way he's leaving until he's damn good and ready. So it looks like it's the town versus the marshal in a fight to the finish... and neither side is going to play by the rules!

Conley is "in the ranks of N. Scott Momaday, Louise Erdrich, James Welch or W. P. Kinsella."
—*The Fort Worth Star-Telegram*

ISBN 13: 978-0-8439-6077-8

FIRST TIME IN PRINT!

OUTLAWS
PAUL BAGDON

Spur Award Finalist and Author of
Deserter and *Bronc Man*

Pound Taylor has just escaped from jail—and the hangman's noose—and he's eager to get back on the outlaw trail. For his gang he chooses his former cell-mate and the father and brothers of his old partner, Zeb Stone. Pound wants to do things right, with lots of planning and minimum gunplay, but the Stone boys figure they can shoot first and worry about the repercussions later. Sure enough, that's just what they do—and they kill a man in the process. With the law breathing down their necks and the whole gang at one another's throats, Pound can see that hangman's noose getting closer all the time. Unless his friends kill him first!

ISBN 13: 978-0-8439-6073-0

LOUIS L'AMOUR

For millions of readers, the name Louis L'Amour is synonymous with the excitement of the Old West. But for too long, many of these tales have only been available in revised, altered versions, often very different from their original form. Here, collected together in paperback for the first time, are four of L'Amour's finest stories, all carefully restored to their initial magazine publication versions.

BIG MEDICINE

This collection includes L'Amour's wonderful short novel *Showdown on the Hogback*, an unforgettable story of ranchers uniting to fight back against the company that's trying to drive them off their land. "Big Medicine" pits a lone prospector against a band of nine Apaches. In "Trail to Pie Town," a man has to get out of town fast after a gunfight leaves his opponent dead on a saloon floor. And the title character in "McQueen of the Tumbling K" is out for revenge after gunmen ambush him and leave him to die.

ISBN 13: 978-0-8439-6068-6

The Classic Film Collection

The Searchers by Alan LeMay

Hailed as one of the greatest American films, *The Searchers,* directed by John Ford and starring John Wayne, has had a direct influence on the works of Martin Scorsese, Steven Spielberg, and many others. Its gorgeous cinematic scope and deeply nuanced characters have proven timeless. And now available for the first time in decades is the powerful novel that inspired this iconic movie. (Coming February 2009!)

Destry Rides Again by Max Brand

Made in 1939, the Golden Year of Hollywood, *Destry Rides Again* helped launch Jimmy Stewart's career and made Marlene Dietrich an American icon. Now available for the first time in decades is the novel that inspired this much-loved movie. (Coming March 2009!)

The Man from Laramie by T. T. Flynn

In its original publication, *The Man from Laramie* had more than half a million copies in print. Shortly thereafter, it became one of the most recognized of the Anthony Mann/Jimmy Stewart collaborations, known for darker films with morally complex characters. Now the novel upon which this classic movie was based is once again available—for the first time in more than fifty years. (Coming April 2009!)

The Unforgiven by Alan LeMay

In this epic American novel, which served as the basis for the classic film directed by John Huston and starring Burt Lancaster and Audrey Hepburn, a family is torn apart when an old enemy starts a vicious rumor that sets the range aflame. Don't miss the powerful novel that inspired the film the *Motion Picture Herald* calls "an absorbing and compelling drama of epic proportions." (Coming May 2009!)

To order a book or to request a catalog call:
1-800-481-9191
Books are also available at your local bookstore, or you can check out our Web site **www.dorchesterpub.com**.